CONFRONTATION

From the closed-circuit TV screen, Lilgin's face looked out at Higenroth. The Dictator smiled cynically.

'Professor, it has been proved that men talk under pressure. Your wife, now . . . she's very attractive. Not too long ago, Professor, a man wouldn't tell us his secrets. We had his wife torn to pieces before his eyes. He talked. We think that you will talk as it starts to happen to a wife who is expecting your child.'

Higenroth held his breath. How would this creature react, he wondered, when he discovered what pressure *he* was already under? Any moment now . . .

As if the expectation were a signal, there was a muffled cry from somewhere behind Higenroth. One of the Dictator's aides was sitting up; he wore earphones.

The man screeched, 'Your excellency, this scene – what you're doing and saying here – is being broadcast everywhere!'

Also by A. E. Van Vogt in Sphere Science Fiction:

MISSION TO THE STARS
THE WORLD OF NULL-A
THE PAWNS OF NULL-A
THE SECRET GALACTICS
THE UNIVERSE MAKER
THE BEST OF A. E. VAN VOGT

Tyranopolis

A. E. VAN VOGT

SPHERE BOOKS LIMITED
30/32 Gray's Inn Road, London WC1X 8JL

First published in Great Britain under the title ***Future Glitter*** by Sidgwick & Jackson Ltd. 1976

First Sphere Books edition 1977

Filmset in Photon Plantin

Printed in Great Britain by
C. Nicholls & Company Ltd
The Philips Park Press, Manchester

AUTHOR'S INTRODUCTION

In mid-January, 1972, a super-talented friend of mine, Sam Locke, phoned me and said in a hushed voice, 'I have just had a phone call from someone I went to school with, and who disappeared in 1947.' Sam writes for TV and films, has had a play produced on Broadway, and has been a co-author on five Broadway musicals. His long lost school chum was one of those army casualties. He was taught to speak Chinese, and then, of course he was sent to France.

It turns out that in 1947 he decided to visit China. While in Shanghai he married a Chinese girl, and was still there when the Communists took over in '49.

In 1971 he accompanied the Red China mission to the U.N. Naturally, he looked up his old friends. He wanted to fly out from New York, and 'have one of those dinners your mother used to cook.' That part would be private. But after the dinner Sam wanted to invite a few people to meet his former friend, and (he said), 'Although I know you're a Republican at heart, though you claim to be a registered Democrat, would you like to be one of the guests?'

(For the record, I'm a middle liberal without a leftist bone in my body; or a rightist bone. And I know what that means).

I said, 'Sam, I'm one of the people who absolutely should be at that party; since I am an intellectual expert on Red China, and have written a researched novel on the subject.'

. . . In case you wonder why I'm telling this anecdote, the dictator in this story, TYRANOPOLIS, is a 23rd century parallel to the career and character of the Russian despot, Joseph Stalin. The background of that future state also has elements in it of the China of Mao Tse-tung, the Chinese Communist leader. What I wish to establish is that I am qualified to do such a parallel.

My Red China novel, THE VIOLENT MAN (not science fiction) was published in 1962 by Farrar, Straus and Giroux, and subsequently ran through five Avon paperback printings. It took eight years to write. To write it, I read and reread approximately 100 books on China and Communism. At that time I learned the painful lesson of the student who does not underline salient points. Thus, in preparation for TYRANOPOLIS, I read, and underlined, KHRUSHCHEV REMEMBERS, Medvedev's LET HISTORY JUDGE, and, for the picture of scientists in prison, Solzhenitsyn's THE FIRST CIRCLE.

How did all this work out for me at Sam Locke's party? Well, it turned out that Sam's 'few people' consisted of about fifty individuals, most of whom were crowded around the guest of honour. He sat on a couch, and every seat near him was occupied. I did one of my system things. I settled down in a chair at the remote outskirts of this group. Whenever someone got up – which they did to get a drink, or whatever – I either got that chair; or, if someone else got it first, I took his. By this method, in approximately one hour I was sitting next to the only white man who accompanied the Red Chinese mission to the U.N.

I clung there approximately one hour; and, despite interruptions, I asked my questions.

Here are samples: 'What is the dust situation in Peking today?' ('Solved,' he answered.) 'Are the Chinese still spitting on sidewalks, in railroad cars, everywhere?' ('No. The spitting problem was solved with millions of spittoons and psychological pressure – and that ended the common cold as a national calamity.) 'What level of relationship is permitted between older boys and girls?' ('The situation is terrible,' he said. 'Because of the population thing, the pressure on the kids is so great, they virtually do not dare to speak to each other.')

You may ask, did I believe his answers? Was the dust problem in Peking solved? (Starting about 75 years ago, Peking became, progressively, a dustier city. It even 'snowed' dust in winter. It was believed that wind shifts brought dust from the Gobi desert to this unhappy city. The Communist solution was to replant trees in strategic areas, so this gentleman said. When Nixon visited Peking, I looked for the trees, and there they were.)

We must remember that dictators can often solve problems by fiat. My dictator (in TYRANOPOLIS) created a 'perfect' world. You'll have to decide for yourself if you care to pay the price of solutions by such a method.

Later in the evening, when I went over to Sam's friend to say goodbye, he said, 'You're the only person I've met in the U.S. who knows anything about China. Why don't you come and visit me in Peking when relations between the U.S. and China are normalized?'

Obviously, his was over-praise. There are in this country, academic experts, journalist experts, diplomatic experts, *and* people (like the late Henry Luce) who were born in China. Many of these, including a White Russian woman I know in Oregon, even speak the language fluently.

But I was in my time an intellectual expert. That is, a writer who took the laborious trouble to get his facts straight.

The same applies to all Communist references in TYRANOPOLIS, and to the entire psychology quoted or paraphrased in various parts of the story. Anti-communists, who somehow have thought of the whole pack of early Russian and Chinese Reds as gangs of semi-literate hill bandits, will be surprised to discover that they were intellectuals who had their own extensive terminology, which they understood perfectly. And which is used in my novel without so much as the alteration of a single letter.

In order to dramatize what might seem 'heavy' stuff, I decided on a very bizarre opening sequence, and to continue with other bizarre techniques. The result is a far-out fantastic novel without a visible trace of intellectuality.

But it's there.

ONE

Professor Dun Higenroth read the official letter with pursed lips:

'. . . Your good fortune to have won the Accolade for your field . . . Hence, your decapitation on behalf of your students in the advanced educational programme . . . will take place on Patriotic Day. Congratulations . . .'

There was more, but that was the gist.

Silently, Higenroth handed the document across the breakfast table to his wife,. Eidy. For no clear reason, he watched closely as that young lady read the news of the imminent beheading of her elderly husband, but she showed no visible emotion. She handed the paper back, and said, 'The important thing to remember is that beheading doesn't hurt. That's been proved.'

Higenroth discovered as he now read the fine print, that there was a footnote about that very subject in the execution order:

'. . . It is taken for granted that the Accolade winner will not allow anxiety about the actual moment of decapitation to show in his behaviour or be of any concern in his thoughts. Such old-style reactions are not for the modern, mature scientist, who understands the value of Accolade beheading to his students and knows that for him it is a step from this world into a better one, as has been established by the Official Religion.'

The award confronted Professor Higenroth with a dilemma. On the one hand – he had to admit it – it was a victory. His long battle with Dr. Heen Glucken had ended in a clean cut – so to say – knockout of his adversary. Accolade winners were clearly demarcated front runners in the struggle for scientific eminence.

In a single stroke – literally speaking – he would win the crown.

On the other hand, he did not quite feel that his work was done. 'There's still a lot of creativity in the old noodle,' he said to Eidy. 'And so I think I'll ask for an indefinite postponement on the grounds of Future Glitter.'

Eidy said, 'You don't think this has anything to do with those political writings you've been publishing for two years against the regime?'

'Oh, no.' Higenroth shook his lean head. 'The dictator has definitely stated that all viewpoints will be tolerated. The possibility that the Accolade is not earned is not a factor in the matter.'

'Of course,' said Eidy hastily.

Since Patriotic Day was only half a week distant, Higenroth made his application for postponement on a form provided and sent it to the Board of Advanced Education by magnetic jet special delivery.

The news of his award was on the morning telews. Early the next day, Dr. Glucken jetted in from overseas, as he put it, 'to pay my final respects to a worthy opponent.' He added, 'I cannot say that I fully accept their judgement, but I think I have a solution that will satisfy me.'

He thereupon launched into a summary of his own views.

For some reason that he could not explain, Higenroth had not slept well; and so it was a little while before he alerted sufficiently to a realization that Dr. Glucken was off on the same old tiresome subject of airing his private theories.

'. . . It would be a scientific triumph,' Glucken was saying, 'if your students at the time of decapitation not only received a flash of education in all of your special knowledge but also of mine.'

As the eager voice continued, Higenroth began to stir. Suddenly, he was galvanized. 'Just a moment,' he said. 'Are you suggesting? –'

Glucken went on with his presentation of certain basic theories, merely raising his voice.

Higenroth came more awake. 'Hey!' he said. 'Are you trying to ensure that *my* students are educated in *your* ideas when *I* am decapitated?'

Glucken continued his summation, talking even louder.

Higenroth placed his hands over his ears and shouted that he would be damned if he would allow the Accolade Committee's judgement to be perverted by ideas that were not of Accolade stature.

At this point, Eidy came rushing in. She hurriedly led her

husband out of the room, but the two men yelled at each other until she had successfully shoved the professor through the door of his bedroom and closed the door.

Dr. Glucken, his lean, rather good-looking face red, was on the point of leaving the house when Eidy came hurrying back. She stopped him at the door.

'Are you married?' she asked.

'My wife is dead,' he replied. 'She questioned the Official Religion.' He shrugged. 'I warned her.'

Eidy knew what he meant. That was the one forbidden action in an otherwise benign dictatorship.

What troubled her now was that she had married Higenroth when she was still one of his students under a government programme in which attractive teen-age girls were patriotically wed to famous scientists. Once a girl had been patriotic in this fashion she was usually expected to continue, and it seemed to her that Dr. Glucken was quite an attractive male for a scientist. And since he would be the unquestioned Number One in the field after the decapitation of her present husband, she now simpered a little as she shook his lean hand, holding it longer than was necessary. Then she drew back and waited anxiously, for this was a marriage she might be interested in. If this failed, who knew who she would get – another Higenroth?

But Dr. Glucken was inwardly shaking his head over the thought that had fleetingly come into his mind, also. The feeling was particularly strong for a moment as he noticed – he couldn't help but notice – what an unusually pretty girl she was. But such a marriage might be taken as a sign of surrender on his part to Higenroth's ideas, which of course could never be.

The sound of the doorbell shortly after the departure of Dr. Glucken brought traditional battlers into the house: Professor Higenroth's students. Eidy, who opened the door, was smashed against one wall by a surging mass of young male and female bodies as, squealing, they poured past her, seeking their mentor.

The professor had emerged from the bedroom and had stripped himself for the bathtub. He half-turned, startled, when the first lapping pulse of the tidal wave of students – who were still pouring through the front door – caught him and swept him into the adjoining hallway; and so, battered but still alive, to the patio beyond. There, he was quickly tumbled to the grass.

A pair of clippers was produced. His hair was sheared off by this efficient instrument. Next, his head was shaved. While this transpired, he was aware that a raffle was being conducted, with two girls and two boys acting as arbiters. The raffle would decide which students won the ten choice positions on the professor's valuable head.

The scientific study of the educational value of decapitation had resulted from an old folk observation: Gradually, after death, a human face ceases to look the way it did when alive. Family resemblance disappears. A stranger lies on the slab, in the coffin, in the ground.

Scientific investigators, working for the dictator – under a directive to seek ever new ways for transmitting knowledge to the younger generation – determined that the dead body, particularly the massively charged-up head, gradually loses its lifetime accumulation of information and conditioning. Normally, this simply drains off into the air. But tests demonstrated that the energy pulses could be drawn off into the heads of students by means of proper electrical connections. It was discovered – so it was claimed – that, when suddenly decapitated, the head released about 70% of its burden within a few minutes.

Thus the science of educational beheading was born under the firm directive of a farseeing dictatorship. In addition to its strictly utilitarian purpose, the method had become a means of giving recognition for meritorious scientific achievements to many persons who, because of their anti-government writings and activities, might never have been recommended for honours by over-zealous government agencies, smarting under criticism. This limitation on the part of loyal henchmen was recognized by the dictator, and – as he put it – the most useful redress made.

The student battle for head position had become an old tradition. And so, after his first startled reaction, Professor Higenroth submitted goodnaturedly to the minor indignities involved: a bloody scalp and a dizzy sense of having been battered by innumerable blunt instruments.

And, when they departed, he came to the door and cheerfully waved them goodbye.

On the morning after his second sleepless night, Professor

Higenroth confessed to Eidy that for some reason, which was not clear to him, he was feeling concern about the moment of decapitation. All through the night – he reported – he had been literally haunted by endless images, which implied some kind of internal resistance to receiving the Accolade. In fact, he had even had fleeting moments when he found himself rejecting the Official Religion, with all its pleasant reassurances.

'If this goes on,' he said, 'I may disgrace you by taking to my heels during this final night and heading for the Hills.'

The 'Hills' was a euphemism. The word referred to the anti-government forces who – it was rumoured – had their strongholds in great, fortified mountain regions. The rumour, Higenroth knew, was false. Modern arms made a physical redoubt anywhere on the planet unfeasible.

He saw that his words had quite properly alarmed Eidy. If an Accolade winner failed to show up at the block on Patriotic Day – tomorrow – a near relative substituted for him. The substitution had no educational value. It was merely a custom, designed according to official doctrine 'to save the honour of the family, who naturally will not want to lose the Accolade.'

Since it was taken for granted that each family member would want such an honour for himself – of being the substitute – to prevent squabbling, an order of precedence had been established by decree: wife, father, mother, eldest brother, eldest sister, and so on. Children were exempted because the regime loved all children. However, if there were no near relatives, the next leading scientific contender for the Accolade fulfilled the honour.

Since Higenroth had only Eidy, Heen Glucken would come right after her. The young woman's situation was complicated by an unfortunate event that had occurred shortly after her marriage to Higenroth. At that time she had put a lock on her door and informed him that for some reason she had no interest in the man–woman relationship.

It was late afternoon when Eidy appeared in her husband's bedroom without any clothes on and reported to him that the prospect of losing him had stimulated her to a great admiration for his manly qualities. She was accordingly – she said – his 'to do with as you will.'

Whereupon, she laid herself down on his bed.

Professor Higenroth gazed at her girlish figure for a long moment. Then he walked over to a chair by the window and abruptly sat down.

A fantastic thought had flashed through his mind for the first time, the very first time: 'This is why I did all this.'

He stared, wondering at himself, through the window glass at the green campus grounds beyond.

'Well, here it is,' he thought. 'Success.'

Here was the end result of his feverish behaviour of the past two years: the subconscious scheme to capture her and her affections at no matter what cost. That was the picture he suddenly saw.

'They got me!' he thought. And it was justice that they had. Not their justice, but his own inner truth kind. His crime: an elderly male agreeing to let a teen-age girl be forced to marry him.

Yet, after a little, his agreement with the punishment yielded to amazement at how much pressure it had taken to break down the resistance of this slip of a girl.

Once more, he went over to where she lay, looked down at her naked girlish body, and was ashamed of himself. Though, now that he could think again, it occurred to him that her intended role at this instant was equally shameful.

Not once had she shown concern. And here she was, determined – he realized – to hold him for the executioner's axe. At this penultimate moment, no price evidently was too high, including delivery of the sex she had hitherto denied him.

And so his question to himself was: did either Glucken or she or he himself deserve mercy? He couldn't decide. So – without a word – he turned, left the room, locked the door behind him.

He went to his den. Everything inside his skin felt different. His mind was working again in a reasoning way, as if released from a timeless thrall. And so, as he sat down before what seemed to be a blank wall, he was keenly aware of many logical possibilities.

As he gazed at the wall, a picture appeared on it. Of Eidy at the phone about an hour earlier, putting through a long distance call to Dr. Heen Glucken. Her voice, as she talked, came clear and pure from a hidden speaker. Dr. Glucken's progressively alarmed voice came equally clear, undistorted despite that it was coming from across the ocean.

Higenroth listened with a faraway look in his eyes as Eidy told Glucken of her husband's remark about taking to the Hills. 'You know what that means,' she spelled out for her distant listener. 'If he gets away, I'm next. And if I go with him, you're next.'

She added plaintively, 'I don't want to go to the Hills. I don't want to leave civilization.'

Higenroth shook his head wonderingly at the word. 'She calls *this*, civilization!' he thought. 'The world of a tyrant whose like has not been seen since –'

He couldn't imagine a comparison. Yet, fact was until his marriage to Eidy he had held still for the rigidities of the system, because he had a philosophy of his own about the hard necessities of transitional periods in history.

. . . He grew aware that Eidy had made her point, for Dr. Glucken agreed he would marry her after the Accolade award was achieved for Higenroth, and agreed to make all the necessary contacts with the Board of Education to ensure that the professor kept his Accolade appointment.

And Eidy agreed to hold her husband by every possible means until the ultimate moment – at which time, of course, he would be picked up by the authorities.

Dr. Glucken next asked Eidy if she had a clue for him as to the direction of Higenroth's theories of the past ten years. 'He achieved that breakthrough whereby distance, no matter how great, can invariably be made to equal zero – we're talking on that system now; notice how completely natural our voices sound! But since then he seems to have been puttering around perfecting aspects of that. I can't believe that's all he's been up to. He always was a wily so-and-so . . . until he began those anti-government writings.'

A Result of the Eidy Effect, Higenroth thought, sarcastically. It had taken a teen-age girl to knock him out of his good sense.

Watching the perfect image of her on the wall, he saw Eidy shake her head doubtfully, then, 'I came in on him one day by surprise – I was supposed to be shopping – and he had pictures on every wall in the living room, which are just of ordinary plastic. He asked me to forget I had seen them. Is that what you mean?'

Higenroth felt himself turn grey. 'Trust a woman!' he

thought. He should, of course, never have asked her for secrecy.

'Hey!' said Dr. Glucken, 'that sounds like his early discredited Pervasive Theory. If he's found a way through that! –' His voice went up half an octave, 'This should get me a hearing from the dictator himself.'

He thereupon impressed on the girl the importance of making an effort during these final hours to obtain further information about Higenroth's communication theories. Eidy promised to do so.

It did not seem to occur to either – Higenroth observed wryly – that, according to the mystique of Accolade beheading, the information would be passed on to Higenroth's students.

The trans-oceanic conversation ended with Eidy saying urgently that she had been greatly attracted to Glucken; and the doctor gallantly responded with a confession of strong attraction on his part, also.

On the wall scene, Eidy replaced the receiver, stood up, and walked off through a door.

Higenroth's communication system could have followed her; for every wall in this house was automatically a pick-up stimulator. But two feelings were struggling to take over his mind.

The first – to solve the problem of escape.

The second, more powerful, was a male impulse. This time, conscious.

At the time of the marriage, he had pretended to himself that he had no control over the matter; that if the government saw fit to present him with a beautiful wife, how could he stop them? He who was not openly resisting the dictatorship.

All that had to go. It was an inner lie – from which he must separate himself forever. In a way it was ridiculous that a beautiful young human female was willing to move over to another man for the reasons that were now motivating Eidy.

But that didn't matter. None of his business what she did in the future with that perfect skin and those shapely bones.

TWO

The Higenroth Matter found the Dictator's Court in the throes of a typical score of madnesses. Two of the Great Man's three current mistresses were in process of being 'phased out'; and each of the discards was being difficult about it in her own way. The duo of replacements were still in that state of being insanely proud. For them, it was too early for the realization that, statistically, a woman spent slightly less than five months in the 'king's' bed.

Because of these and other personal matters, it was a problem time for top government aides. As one whose status was unofficially number fourteen (because he was sincere) said to another who was at least Number Three, 'I recalled Higenroth to him earlier this evening. For a few moments he didn't remember the name. Then he said, "Oh, yes – the communications fellow. When does that come up?"

'"It's up, Sire," I said. "Higenroth is to be beheaded tomorrow." "Oh," he replied, "what was our decision about that?" "Your excellency," I answered him, "this man is believed to be in possession of scientific information of an advanced nature." "Oh, yes, didn't I interview another communications expert about that yesterday?" "Herr Doctor Glucken," I prompted him. "Of course," he said. "So it's all settled. There will be a confrontation. So – very well done. Goodbye for now." And he walked on, smiling that smile of his.'

The two men had met in the hall of mirrors. Number Fourteen was a muscular young man in his thirties, whose name was Crother Williams. He had troubled grey eyes and was officially labelled a scientific intellectual. The other man, Number Three, was older, taller, leaner. His name was Appiter Jodell, and he was a political intellectual. It was he who spoke next, with a faintly sly smile.

'My friend,' he said, 'The Boss plays these little games with you because he's noticed that his apparent memory lapses confuse you. He enjoys your uncertainty.'

'That's what you keep saying,' said Williams unhappily. 'Can you tell me what his various statements meant?'

'It's simple. His Alter Ego will talk to Higenroth via closed circuit TV some time after midnight tonight.'

'Why not him talk to Higenroth?'

'Because, my friend, he spoke objectively. He said, as you reported it, "There will be a confrontation." That is what he said, isn't it?'

Number Fourteen sighed. 'Does the Alter Ego know what he's supposed to say?'

'He'd better know. And since he's been around longer than most Alters, he'll probably wiggle through.'

'To what conclusion?'

'Well, you reason it out. The ideal would be – Higenroth hands over his secret science, and dies on the block tomorrow. Perfect solution, right?'

'But why would he hand it over?'

'That's *your* job.'

'For God's sake, how and when did I get that as an assignment?'

'You were the one that somehow – it was no accident, I assure you – happened to meet The Boss in that doorway this evening.'

The expression on the younger man's face reflected a combination of amazement and dismay. Twice, he tried to speak, but all he could manage each time was a gulp.

Number Three continued, in a decisive tone, 'He'll expect a Total Victory report from you and the Alter Ego tomorrow.' The older man started to walk past Williams, paused, turned, and said casually, 'Your meeting me here was no accident either. The Boss had the feeling you weren't picking up his message; and he called me a few minutes ago. Better get on it, sir.'

THREE

Late afternoon of the day prior to the beheading, Higenroth was still considering alternatives.

And, in fact – he analyzed – they would expect it. Would be suspicious if he failed to make obvious attempts at survival ... Might as well go through the stereotyped motions – he told himself cynically.

He had been sitting in a chair in the patio, warming himself in the sun. Without moving, and using the concrete wall of the patio directly in front of him as a reflector – let them figure that out (if they were watching) – he mentally activated his pervasive system, and located a Hills Adviser. Higenroth seemed, then, to speak directly into the air in front of him, but actually his voice was picked up by a tiny microphone in the make-up at the tip of his nose. The Adviser's image was on the wall. He listened with pursed lips to Higenroth's dilemma, and finally shook his head.

'As soon as your wife realizes The Hills have no specific location, she'll betray you at one of your Restovers. So—no—do not bring her along.'

A Restover – it was widely believed – was the home of a Hills sympathizer, who would put up a Wanted for two weeks, then pass him on to another Restover. Higenroth knew better. 'The Hills' was a government organization with an elaborate system for dealing with rebels, escapees, and other establishment opponents.

The dissidents always ended up dead or captured, but seldom right away. The authorities took pains to make sure that, although the victim was never out of their control, he always thought he was safe. And, when he was finally cornered, they tried to arrange it so that he believed he was victim of an accidental exposure or of an error that he personally had made.

What made The Hills attractive to Higenroth on this fateful afternoon was the possibility that the figures on Eidy's calendar did not mean what he had always believed, and that therefore in order to achieve his long-run purpose, he would need to delay his execution a week or so.

The Adviser was urging, 'Why don't we pick you up about 3 A.M. and take you to a Restover. Leave your wife locked in the bedroom. After all, you're the scientist, the important one.'

Higenroth parried, 'Remember, she's a victim, also. Maybe there's a better solution. Let me think about it.'

'Don't wait too long!' the Adviser warned.

Higenroth felt a fleeting admiration. It was amazing that an Adviser need show no cunning; but could simply and instantly give honest opinions. The spokesman of a genuine rebel organization could have said no better than this somewhat plump, earnest, youngish man.

He broke the connection, abruptly more cheerful. System perfection almost always had an energizing effect on him . . . Let's face it, he decided, I'm sixty-eight. My job is not to save myself but to save the pervasive system – so that at a future time a younger man than himself could use it to solve the problem of an all-powerful dictatorship that had twice now successfully passed on the mantle of power.

The earth was ruled by a third generation dictatorship – which indicated that a method had at last been found for training a political heir. Of itself that was a unique event, worth special study.

Only the king system, or certain types of elective systems, had previously been able to achieve similar bloodless inheritance of power; not that there wasn't always some bloodshed, probably more than was known. Higenroth had his own unspoken views on the matter.

Question: what younger man should he select for the task?

Regretfully, he rejected his students as possibilities. It was regretful because two of the girls and one of the boys were unusually bright people. They would all – all – be suspects, and would probably be executed. Every single one, boys and girls. If there was hope for them, it would be because he meticulously avoided contact in these final hours.

No, no, he thought, there was – now that he had considered it – only one remote possibility. Maybe fate was on his side after all.

He stood up, smiling faintly, and returned to the bedroom. Eidy had drawn the covers over her body and her young face was fear-ridden. 'Why did you lock me in?' she asked in a trembling tone.

'I didn't want you to leave,' he replied.

Her expression changed. It struck Higenroth that she must consider him out of his mind. Obviously, he couldn't drive her away with a whip at this stage.

Higenroth sat down on the bed beside her. 'What time of the month is this for you? Are you likely to become pregnant?'

'But I want to.' She must instantly have thought he had a hope about it. Because in a flash she had flung the covers aside; and, nude body gleaming, she was off to her own room. She came racing back with a calendar on which her menstrual periods were marked in red circles. And no question, it was what he had believed – today was the virtual middle of the menstrual month – the fertile period.

Well-l-l-ll, thought Higenroth, we don't have to do anything complex like fleeing to a Restover . . . It was all here, the time, the woman, the state of mind. Today, it was her task to hold him, and it was his to save the world at some future time by taking advantage of the pressure she was under.

Not exactly an ideal time for sex; his attention kept being distracted. Yet in the end he managed a creditable performance, and so had his first carnal knowledge of his lawfully wedded wife. It was, he told himself, a legal act between two legally associated human beings, and not merely a matter of consenting adults; though that factor was also present.

Eidy stayed with him the remainder of the afternoon, and placed what amounted to a stranglehold on him the early part of the evening. Shortly before ten (which hour was normally her bedtime), he began to tell her about his invention. It was a calculated act on his part. He had long ago observed that any talk of science could put Eidy to sleep faster than sleeping pills.

As he had anticipated, even now when she wanted to hear, she yawned repeatedly as he talked:

. . . Those other fools dismissed the problem as insoluble. They said, the idiots. . .' Higenroth could not restrain his scorn '. . . that sound and light waves damp out in seconds . . . Now, of course, that's true at some levels. It's not true on others. What they forgot is that there's energy everywhere, and a carrier wave can utilize what's at any spot for amplification and relay. I can send a message any distance. And what Glucken doesn't know is, I don't need a receiver at the other end . . .'

A faint, faint snore answered him.

Higenroth eased himself out of the bed, took his clothes down the hall, dressed – and came back to her, wheeling his machine over to where the troubled girl lay in an exhausted sleep. He focused the projector on the part of her body where, now, eight hours after the first intercourse, the sperm would have penetrated the ovum. Watched until a needle moved slightly. Then locked it in place.

The tiny bio-structure that would at some future time be a human being, was his victim – Who else? What else? The truth was, it was the only way any child of his would survive: if that madman in the palace believed that somewhere in the baby, the toddler, the child, the teen-ager, was in fact the information about the pervasive system. Even – Higenroth speculated – Eidy might be allowed to live out her life this way.

There was no other hope for her; of that he was sure.

There was no dissembling now. He presumed that spy rays were trying to see and hear what went on in this house. But of course that was his field of mastery. As he softly spoke his truth in a soundproofed microphone and by that means into the field that he had set up around the newly created embryo, unpenetrable interference barred not only the avid listeners and viewers who were out there, but also Eidy's ears.

No chance, now, of her being later hypnotized and the words evoked from her subconscious.

The delicate task completed, he removed the key circuit from the projection machine and ground it to nothing under his heel. Then he headed back to his den. Now that the critical hour of midnight was approaching . . . time he checked out that the enemy had indeed been observing him.

FOUR

Over at the enemy, where the power was, hordes of experts under Fourteen's direction, had been busy. They were thinking, planning, re-examining Higenroth's file from A to Z. While he was in bed with Eidy, committees considered just about every possibility of the situation.

Suppose he had nothing? they asked.

Then why wasn't he fleeing to The Hills – that sticky little trap for foolish rebels, who actually believed there was a place to escape to?

But, again, if he had something – what a pressure that

possibility created. It was the pressure experienced by a type of human being who excelled in one peculiar ability: how fast could he come to heel, how swiftly could he find a solution that would assuage the dictator, how abjectly could he then fall over other peculiars like himself in his eagerness to help kill, wound, or damage the doomed person.

Even Crother Williams – Number Fourteen – had some of that anxiety. What he did not share, or even really suspect in them, was their mindless willingness to do anything against the selected victim. His intent: We will do tonight what is necessary. And let the law handle the rest, as already prescribed. Meaning, the Accolade beheading process was their final solution, if all else failed.

By midnight, under Williams' direction, a small army of men and an enormous technological array was moving in upon the little university town, concentrating the power of the State against one man.

Higenroth's check-out first showed on his den wall the outline of a big ship high in the night sky above his house. Within instants his perfect system was surveying the interior of what he recognized as a police laboratory vessel. What startled Higenroth, however, was the enormous armament of the ship.

'Hey!' he thought, 'that's a cover ship.'

Covering somebody's approach to his house, or making sure he didn't escape, Higenroth made a quick examination of the craft's equipment, nodded his head with reluctant admiration – they were loaded for a total overwhelm of his pervasive transmission system.

Belatedly, he saw that Dr. Glucken was one of the scientists at the massive instrument board.

That one clue, Higenroth thought, his colour draining. Glucken had not, of course, analyzed the secrets of the pervasive system. But he was sitting up there now, ready to use the resources of a planet to find out.

Well-l-ll, Higenroth decided finally, I never expected it'd be easy.

He hoped Glucken had got an eyeful of his future bride in bed. One could anticipate that in the Scientific Age people adjusted to such memories at the velocity of fear.

A picture formed on the wall; apprized Higenroth that trucks and men were approaching the house. Hurriedly, he twisted dials that would bar loud sounds from Eidy's room. It was only moments later that the front door crashed with a splintering roar.

As men grabbed him, Higenroth recognized Fourteen. Instantly, the older man ceased his mild struggling, and offered the other a faint, almost sympathetic smile. 'Do what's right,' he said. 'You'll feel better.'

The younger man gave him a startled glance. Then he stiffened. 'The law is right,' he said harshly. 'The law requires all scientific secrets to be revealed. There are no exceptions, not even Professor Higenroth.'

The scientist pursed his lips. 'I was wondering how a man like you would work out a moral dilemma inside himself. And that one is pretty good.'

'Do you suggest –' Fourteen spoke grimly '– that the law is wrong? Do you imply that the system which now exists, is in error? Do you question the right of Lilgin to rule in the world as it is today, barely out of anarchy?'

It was the kind of argument that had no future. So Higenroth cut past it. 'Frankly,' he said, 'I'd like to get out of the mess I'm in. But I understand that his excellency does not make deals with condemned persons.'

'It's impossible,' was the stiff reply. 'It's too late.'

'Then all I can say,' said Higenroth, 'is, if you have been assigned the task of obtaining non-existent information from me, without having the power to offer me anything in return, well, then, young man, you're in as big a mess as I am.'

'You're implying,' said Williams, 'that there's no rationality in what is happening. I assure you it is completely logical.'

He did not wait for a reply but spun on his heels, and said curtly, 'Bring it in here!'

What was brought in was a closed circuit television set of an advanced design. Higenroth stared at the machine, suddenly hopeful. He said to Fourteen, 'Maybe you were too hasty in your judgement. Maybe there will be a transaction. Maybe –'

He stopped. For on the viewplate of the set there was a brightness, which resolved into the eidolon of the most famous face of all. Seeing it, the lesser officials in the room dived ingratiatingly to the floor. Fourteen remained standing. And Higenroth's guards held him, and themselves remained erect; merely raised their eyes towards the ceiling in a soldierly respect.

After one prolonged look into those metal-like black eyes, Higenroth wondered: Well-l-ll, is it the Egotist himself, or his Alter Ego? Since it was *the* face, it was a fantastic achievement either way. The Great Man knew. Surely, they wouldn't use his double without his express permission.

Even that didn't matter.

By bringing in the TV, they were temporarily opening up their energy barriers. That mattered.

On the screen, the lips parted. The famous, resonant baritone voice said: 'From you, Professor, we now require, for the people, a total revelation of your pervasive system.'

Higenroth was intently concentrating on the mental pattern that would, indeed, make this temporary contact a permanent revelation of his system for the people. So he made no reply.

Again, the voice spoke:

'Professor, it has been proved that men talk under pressure. The pressure for you – well, nearly three years ago, my aides were instructed to find the most attractive girl in the world. They found her. She was put into one of your classes. The rest is history.'

No question, they got me!

The moustached, fatherly face – everybody's father – smiled in an unfatherly way; almost a snarl. The voice said cynically (a forbidden emotion; so it must be the Alter Ego):

'I mention this because not too long ago, Professor, a man wouldn't tell us his secrets. We had his wife torn to pieces before his eyes. That he could stand. Then we started on him. That he couldn't stand. He talked. We think that you will talk as it starts to happen to a wife who is expecting your child.'

Higenroth held his breath. How would this creature react, he wondered, when he discovered what pressure *he* was already under – though he didn't know it yet.

But any moment now . . .

As if the expectation were a signal, there was a muffled cry from the floor somewhere behind Higenroth. The old scientist glanced around, and saw that one of the dictator's aides was sitting up; and that he wore earphones.

The man screeched: 'Your excellency, this scene – what you're doing and saying here – is being broadcast everywhere!'

Higenroth suppressed a strong impulse to raise his hand like the precise scholar he was, and correct the statement.

What he wanted to say, was, 'Not broadcast everywhere, but pervasively communicated, sir. Meaning, your lackeyed fool heard it wrong. It's a worse situation than you think, and it won't do any good to shut off that set now.'

It was not necessary to piece together, afterwards, what happened next. Until now, except for this room, the pervasive system had moved in on that closed-circuit television – what a perfect zeroing-in modality that had provided him – located the dictator, patterned him, and was now permanently focused.

Henceforth, every move of the dictator, and every word spoken by him, would emanate from all the plastic walls in the world. Including, as Higenroth mentally made the adjustment – the plastic walls of this room.

So, with the others, he watched as the dictator flung his hand against a switch that disconnected the television. Too late. Then he watched as the dictator, visible against the background of a somewhat larger and more ornate room, hastily stood up and walked over to several men wearing the humble uniform prescribed for top police officers.

One of these men said to him, suavely, 'Your excellency, after all, our purpose has been to discover what advanced science we are dealing with. And so, since in all this great world you are the one person whose life is an open book, therefore it is a wonderful thing that a method has at last been devised whereby you can share yourself with your people everywhere.'

So it is the Alter Ego.

Because he had hoped in a tiny way, when he saw the familiar face, that it might be the dictator in person; and because if it wasn't – if it was in fact the Alter Ego – then Professor Higenroth was as good as dead. His heart sank ever so little.

Almost at once, the old man braced himself. After all, he hadn't really expected to save his own life. Let's continue with the game of rescuing the world in some future time.

It was interesting to watch, in that mood, the dictator's

double head back towards the table. The actor, who looked so sensationally similar to Lilgin, clicked on the closed-circuit television that once more gave him direct connection with Higenroth, and said, 'Professor, how do we shut it off?'

Higenroth felt sorry for the man. I'll try to protect him, he thought – but he doubted if it could be done. The Great Big Killer out there in the palace had his own logic for such matters. The logic was that he took no chances. Ever. Undoubtedly, the Alter Ego would have to be murdered, on the mere possibility that he would remain connected to Higenroth's machine.

Higenroth said, 'I wanted to take this opportunity to show you and the world what a wonderful opportunity for perfect communication now exists between the government and the world. Here in this method is at long last a system whereby a leader's private and public life, every word he speaks, every instruction he gives, what he is like when he is alone, how and with whom he makes love – the entire moment by moment existence of a ruler – shall be visible to all the people all the time. No more secrets, no more need to maintain a public image, no propaganda department – just simply on the walls of everybody's home and office, there he is.

'Naturally,' the old scientist went on, 'it is not my intention to force such a system upon anyone. And in fact I shall shortly shut off the equipment. It is my suggestion that at some later time you will order that it be turned back on. And that, henceforth, of your own free will, you will make this remarkable contact and communication available to the people of this planet.

'And now, in conclusion –' Higenroth continued '– I have an ideal political-economic solution of my own for the world. It is time, in my opinion, that choice be again offered the human race. I urge that the world be divided into two economic areas. One shall be capitalist. The other shall be, uh, a continuation of what we now have. The difference between this idea and what we had in the past would be that there shall be only one political government in charge of both economic areas, making sure that neither encroaches on the other. Ensuring that individuals in both camps may move freely back and forth from one system to the other, as suits their temperaments and momentary interests, all –' he repeated 'under one government.'

As he reached that point, he saw that the face before him had changed. And he thought: they've got what they want, and what I want them to have, a look at my system, and a statement of my purpose. So it was time to say goodbye.

He said it by shaping the particular Alpha wave that shut off the pervasive equipment.

Instantly, the images disappeared from the walls.

On the television the Alter Ego looked relieved. 'Thank you, Professor. And goodbye.'

'Goodbye,' said Higenroth.

As he watched, then, the fateful act that cut him off here, completed. The Alter Ego's hand moved toward the turn-off switch, and touched it.

The image of him faded from the television.

Fourteen came over. 'Well,' he said cheerfully, 'at least now we know the extent of your achievement. And the machinery to do what you have done must be around here somewhere. We need, therefore, only search for it. Or – better still – expect you to be sensible, and show us where it is without fuss.'

That – Higenroth had to admit – was certainly the outward appearance of the situation. It was obvious that even Fourteen was, in effect, saying to himself: with our massive government power, we can move in on this man, Higenroth, and decide from moment to moment what to do with him, since he is completely at our mercy.

The old scientist, observing that attitude, thought wonderingly: they don't seem to realize that they are in my house, and that here I am dictator.

What none of these people comprehended, yet, was that communication is a many-levelled phenomenon. First, of course, there is the communication mode, which can be a voice or an intricate electronic method – and then there was the nervous system, which receives the message.

In the professor's house that last was the principal concern of some of his equipment. To the unnoticing nervous systems of the dictator's dupes, it was presently perfectly logical that they call their huge military trucks and load onto them the machinery that Higenroth located for them behind walls, in hidden basement rooms, and concealed panellings. To the watchers in the big ship above it did seem a little odd that all of the government people crowded into the moving vans, or drove in other cars, and – leaving the Higenroths behind in sole possession of their house – accompanied the captured equipment aboard a huge military transport jet.

Fourteen, using his total authority, contacted the police vessel briefly, and ordered it to continue its watch over the house. Whereupon, the huge plane with himself aboard it, launched itself into the air, and flew off into the darkness.

As soon as the house was clear of intruders – so those aboard the police ship observed with their spy rays – Higenroth went to his wife's bedroom, undressed and retired. In the morning (it was entirely for the benefit of Glucken) the professor once more had carnal knowledge of his attractive young wife. At which time, he began to prepare for the events of Patriotic Day. That was the appearance, and, as it developed, the reality, also.

The past experience of the military watchers aboard the spy ship was that a scientist like Higenroth would go with a silent, faraway look – to the guillotine.

Fourteen was present at the Accolade ceremony, and watched the beheading – which he personally regretted. But, still, this particular scientist had been incredibly foolish: all those critical articles. . . . It was too early for outright antagonists of the government to be allowed. Maybe at some later time, such people could be tolerated. But not now, not yet.

After the deed was done, the youngest member of the Praesidium of the People's Government rounded up the students who had been connected to the professor's knowledgeable – now decapitated – head, and had them all flown to Fortress Ten, a minimum-security prison. The place delusively looked like a country estate; and the young people were temporarily at least delighted with it.

Later in the afternoon, Crother Williams (Number Fourteen) called on Mrs. Higenroth, the new widow. That was shaking. He had heard of her good looks. But after all the palace had its own quota of beautiful women; and so he approached the meeting with Eidy, unprepared.

And stood for many seconds almost blanked out by the breathtaking perfection of her features and matching figure. He managed finally to explain haltingly that the 'uh, government wishes to offer you its protection, and therefore has a temporary home, for you, uh, Mrs. Higenroth . . .'

Where he toc her did look like a home. But it also – like Fortress Ten – was a well-guarded prison.

These tasks completed, Fourteen returned to the palace. And he was indeed very well pleased with himself. He reported to Three, who listened silently to his account, and then said, 'I'll question you in greater detail in the morning. It all seems to have gone too easy.'

'What else could Higenroth do against a large military unit?'

'True,' acknowledged the gaunt man. 'But we'll see in the morning.'

FIVE

As the early dawn light brightened the glazed windows and fine panelled drapes of Fourteen's bedroom, Fourteen's bedside intercom buzzed. He was accustomed to instant awakenings and urgent calls; and so, exhausted though he was, he opened his eyes, reached, and said, 'Williams, sir.'

It was Three phoning from *his* bedroom. 'Jodell here. I have just received a query from the Boss.'

'Yes?' Alertly.

'Where did you have Higenroth's equipment taken?'

'I assumed his excellency wanted it in a near, safe place. So I had it delivered into Storage Room Y-16 in Subbasement Four.'

'You mean, right here in the palace?'

'Yes, sir.'

'Very good. I'll tell him.'

Contact broken, Fourteen settled back into bed with a sleepy sigh – and the intercom buzzed.

He opened his eyes, and saw that it was much brighter outside. So it wasn't really as fast a return call as he had for an instant believed . . . Obviously, I slept.

As before, the face and the speaker on the viewplate was Three. The younger man was startled to see that his senior was fully dressed, and, what was more, very grim.

'I wish to inform you, Mr. Williams, that his excellency requires you to remain in your quarters until this matter of the disappearance of the Higenroth invention is fully cleared up.'

'Uh . . . disappearance?' stuttered Fourteen.

'Earlier this morning, sir, when I informed his excellency of your statement as to the location of the Higenroth equipment, he personally went down to the fourth level basement to storage section Y-16. He discovered that there is no record of delivery.'

Fourteen had an impulse to make another baffled sound. With a gulping effort he restrained himself.

Three was continuing in a taut voice, 'At this moment, sir, it is believed that you were in some way duped by Higenroth. And I am sure you realize that that is the most lenient view that you may hope for. That is all. Disconnect.'

Fourteen sank back into the bed, pale but resigned. He recognized the exact significance of the evaluation made. He was being classified as a fool, which – he realized gloomily – was better than any one of the numerous criminal designations that could have been assigned his negligence.

He could have been labelled a wrecker.

Or a counter-revolutionary.

Or a tool of academic rightists.

Or an ultra-leftist.

Or other diminishments.

The situation was too serious for him to dare remain in bed. Belatedly, he realized that he should have got up right after the first call, and made himself available. That – he deduced now – was what Three must have done.

Hastily, he bathed and shaved, and put on his clothes. And waited. After a while he put in a call for breakfast. It was brought with the usual courtesy. It had been cooked to his taste, and it was served by attentive waiters. Which testified that his disgrace was still a private affair.

As the morning lengthened, Fourteen decided: While I'm waiting, I might as well take care of certain departmental business that I've been holding over for a spare moment.

Which he proceeded to do, by phone and by messenger.

And that also was encouraging. It meant that no attempt was being made as yet to curtail his rights as a member of the Supreme Praesidium . . . So I'll wait patiently. And do as much work as possible . . .

It was pointed out by the investigating committee: on so vast a planet as earth, thousands of events occur every hour. Ships are at sea. Planes are in the air. Trains, buses, cars, people are on the move. And the enormous rocket system for weather, moon, Mars, the asteroids, and other space stations operates on its numerous schedules.

Nobody – it was pointed out – can oppose or take account of so many separate activities, or conceal what he has done once the people that he does control have departed from where he is – not even Higenroth.

So there have to be clues.

That level of reasoning produced a few significant facts. At one of the rocket fields three men were dead, and a rocket was missing.

A number of people were located who had in the line of duty participated in the arrival of the military jet at this rocket field – the jet that carried Crother Williams and other government agents.

But where could the rocket itself have gone? It was presently established that the missing craft was definitely launched. The commission interrogated every connected person who was at that field on that night. During the two weeks of the investigation, the anxious members of the commission got no more than a few hours of restless sleep each night.

After that tense fortnight, they printed their conclusion:

Military Jet NA-6-23-J-271-D was, during the late evening of August 19, 2231 A.D., ordered by Praesidium Member Crother Williams to fly to the home of Professor Dun Higenroth. It settled onto the professor's lawn shortly after midnight, and remained there while unidentified and improperly described equipment was loaded onto it. It then flew to a rocket base, known to government people by the code Hinksa (but publicly called Space Flight Centre 18). There the still undescribed machinery was unloaded into base trucks H-851 and H-327, and transported to the loading platform of rocket repeat type A-J-A 60901. Loaders Malcom Rude and Svely Gruden lifted the equipment up into the freight compartment Storage G-8-T of the rocket, and stored it there. On subsequently being informed that there would be an immediate lift-off, the two men removed the loading platform to its underground safety stall.

In the firing room, the late (murdered) Dal Asher and the late (murdered) Janu Harlitz presumably were informed of the destination of the rocket, and presumably fired the rocket toward that destination, using their programmed systems for doing so, and then erasing the program. The only other person who could have known the destination, the late (murdered) Mathew Arondee, an orbit expert in charge of navigation records for night launches, apparently had those records stolen or destroyed.

According to the evidence of several dozen witnesses, Praesidium Member Crother Williams was the last person to see all of these three (murdered) persons alive.

Subsequently, witnesses reported that Praesidium Member Williams returned to the military jet NA-6, which thereupon flew off and landed in the palace aircraft receiving centre. It remained there until shortly after nine A.M. next morning, at which time Praesidium Member Williams again commandeered it, this time for a flight that carried it and him to the Accolade beheading of Professor Dun Higenroth.

The subsequent movements of this flying machine are on record, but are not relevant to the investigation.

It was pointed out by the investigating group that it had no, and had been given no, authority to request the presence of Praesidium Member Williams at its hearings. And that Praesidium Member Williams did not volunteer to attend any meeting of the investigating commission.

Williams (Fourteen) received a copy of the report in his palace office. When he had read it, pale but brave he called Three and said simply, 'I remember no visit to the rocket field. I presume it happened because Professor Higenroth's invention is missing. I further deduce that all of us who went to Higenroth's house that night were hypnotized by some incredibly powerful mechanical means; and that therefore I should leave the palace at once as I may have had other as yet unknown conditioning – perhaps directed against his excellency. I believe that I should not be hastily disposed of, since I may still be useful in the search. I am willing to be hypnotized extensively for the purpose of obtaining full information from my subconscious. Accordingly, I place myself willingly at either your or his excellency's disposition.'

The voice of Three on the intercom was cool but not unfriendly. 'I have,' he said, 'recorded what you just said. You will be interested to know that it is, in substance, similar to what The Boss said to me after he read the report. My instructions to you are: Do not leave the palace. Do not attend Praesidium meetings. You may go to your office daytimes to conduct your official business, and to your apartment at night. If for any reason your duties require you to be away from the palace, make a request to me and there is already a policy laid down about that. You will be allowed to travel, with permission.'

Three continued, 'You will be extensively hypnotized with a view to obtaining information from you. Later, when Mrs. Higenroth gives birth to Higenroth's child, there's another plan about that which you are to deal with. At the moment the lady is to be hastily wedded to Dr. Glucken, so that he may observe her and question her exhaustively while they are both in the special intimate relation that obtains in the marriage situation. In conclusion . . .'

He paused; and Fourteen said respectfully, 'Yes?'

'It is obvious,' said Three, 'that in view of what has happened, great caution must be exercised. But – let me stress this – there are no punitive intentions. On occasion, The Boss will even talk to you on the intercom. If he does so, under no circumstances are you ever to tell anyone, including me, anything he says to you in such private consultations. Is that understood?'

'Totally.'

Mention of the Higenroth widow had reminded Fourteen of the college students he had transported to Fortress Ten. He brightened as he recalled the fact to Three, and finished, 'After all, we've still got that as an ace in the hole. The data about pervasive theory and practice will also be in their heads.'

There was a pause at the other end of the intercom. The face on the viewplate in Fourteen's office took on a peculiar expression. Something of the meaning of that look penetrated suddenly to Williams, and with it the realization that he had done it again. Despite his very considerable intelligence, he had once more done his naive thing.

He had – he realized his error too late – believed in the given reason for Accolade beheading: that it was in fact a scientifically proved method of transferring information from one brain to another, or others.

He cringed inwardly as the truth struck at him from the older man's expression.

Moments later, Jodell (Three) said scathingly, 'You idiot!' And broke the connection.

SIX

He was young. Only thirty-one.

Being so, and under pressure, Fourteen kept trying to fit the worthy goal into the reality of the political lying that constantly went on around him.

Like so many others, he could see that remorseless logic had its place. Could see that lies seemed to work better than truth with certain groups of people. Therefore, they were a peculiar truth of their own.

If a man will not be swayed to a good action by the simple truth of, for example, that it was a need, but responds, instead, to a falsehood, then that falsehood is *where he is*. There is something deep inside him that can be motivated only by very specific symbols.

Accordingly, you must present him with those exact symbols even though, at first, second, third, and so on glance, they appeared to be contrary to the outward appearance of fact; so reasoned Crother Williams, as others had done before him.

I must, he thought, realize that the good end is what counts. The means would have to be whatever they needed to be.

What it amounted to was adjusting hour by hour to the reality of the reign of Lilgin.

So he took away the boy child when it was born to the beautiful Eidy. On the conscious level, at least, she never knew that the child she was given in return had been born minutes earlier to another young woman.

Similarly, when the second mother later came out of the anaesthetic of her birth-giving time, she gazed at what she was told was her own baby, and felt – well, she had no reason to doubt.

It turned out in later years she was never quite as happy with the baby as she had expected to be. Even as she breast fed it for the very first time, she was sort of fidgety and impatient. Yet despite these half-antagonisms, this mother – whose name was Luena Thomas – did go through certain post-birth stereotypes. She decided that she would indeed name the boy Orlo – after someone on her mother's side of the family.

Eidy thoughtfully named *her* son (at least she accepted that he was her child) with the extremely non-Higenrothian identity, Heen Glucken, Jr.

Her husband, Dr. Glucken, made no comment as this outright falsehood was perpetrated upon him. In his two marriages he had already learned – it seemed to him – that a woman's reality operated more smoothly if, like a river in sand, it was allowed to seek its natural channels, however they might meander from a straight course.

Now, thought Williams, how shall I make sure that the doctors and the nurses and other hospital personnel who may, unknown to me, have observed this switch, do not at some later time feel impelled to reveal the facts to an older Orlo Thomas?

(The Heen Glucken, Jr., side of the swindle was of course politically and scientifically of zero importance.)

In this entire affair, the decisive motivation was provided by a single question: Had an unborn baby been programmed with the knowledge of the pervasive system of communication?

If he had, Orlo Thomas would eventually know what the system was, and perhaps even how to utilize it.

There was, of course, a second question: could the information be filched from Orlo for the benefit of society?

While he considered such details, Praesidium Member Crother Williams occupied a suite of rooms at the Gosindian Hospital. Under his direction, a selected few secret police quietly examined the records of the hospital, altered the necessary documents, and probed the backgrounds of the involved doctors and nurses.

It was all pretty grim. Yet Williams actually lay awake at night striving to think of methods whereby everyone would come through the experience with a whole skin.

The transfers began the first day. Apparently casually. Apparently unrelated to anything that had happened. Presumably, the great mass of hospital personnel had no inkling. The hospital was a ten-thousand-bed monstrosity. It had been purposefully selected for the birth of Eidy's baby because it had the impersonal quality associated with any immense administrative function.

Certain nurses disappeared. Certain doctors were not seen again in their former departments. 'Where's Coduna?' someone would ask. 'Oh, she's now over in Building S. A promotion.' 'Oh, splendid. I'm delighted for her.'

If only that will work, thought Crother Williams, as he lay in the bed in his private apartment, pretending to be a heart case under intensive care.

Uneasy hours passed. Spying devices had been secretly planted on all the people who were now labelled 'suspects'. Day after day, recorders picked up every word they spoke; and Williams had a computer listen to the composite result. It was programmed to select out potentially significant dialogues.

He finally had to admire the total lack of really significant conversation. Without exception, the suspects acted as if they had never heard of Eidy Glucken or Luena Thomas.

Finally, carefully, Williams (Fourteen) reviewed exactly how the babies had been switched. He had personally pretended that he was a minor government official checking hospital facilities. All attendant nurses were ordered out of the room where Eidy's and Luena's babies were two items of several score newborns.

Fourteen went into the deserted (deserted by adults) room. What he did then he had practised beforehand: he removed the identity tags from each baby, switched them, and then switched babies. Then he stood for a long minute looking at all the bits of humanity. After moments only they began to look alike to him.

Surely, doctors and nurses who saw these tiny beings by the hundreds every week, would not suddenly develop an eidetic memory for one or two baby faces.

All right, Williams thought wearily, I've done what I can. To stay any longer would be ridiculous.

Ostensibly, then, he had himself transferred to another hospital. But of course, *en route* his ambulance was diverted to a more practical destination.

He returned to his quarters in the palace, and made his report, and then advised channels that it was available.

And then he waited, uneasily.

Then the phone rang.

It was the secretary of the false front office he had used while acting as the minor official in the hospital. She reported matter-of-factly that she had been contacted by the tearful wife of the doctor who had attended him while he was a false patient.

The doctor had been accidentally killed by a fall from a tenth storey balcony of one of the hospital buildings. The secretary concluded, 'The dead man's wife feels that you and he got so friendly that she was sure you would want to know.'

'Thank you,' said Fourteen automatically, 'send flowers in my name.'

He hung up, pale.

Murder.

The witnesses to the baby switchover were being killed.

For God's sake, he thought, why doesn't he trust me? I could prove to him that those people know nothing.

The 'he' and the 'him' referred exclusively to his excellency, Martin Lilgin, dictator extraordinary.

It seemed to Fourteen that he had taken the most minute care. And in fact the very nature of the message given by the doctor's widow showed no suspicion on her part. Her husband had, of course, unfortunately, told her about the minor government official who was investigating the hospital.

That, Fourteen shook his head over – secrecy is almost impossible, he had to agree – if nowhere else, it was transmitted in the privacy of the bedroom.

Presumably, whatever those nurses and those other doctors and hospital administrative staff suspected (the few who knew of the presence of a minor government official) they would tell it to someone: wife, husband, brother, sister, friend.

Standing there, after disconnecting the instrument, Fourteen thought: They'll all be killed.

He had on one occasion when he was younger – and accepted Lilgin's right to rule with the unquestioning faith of a typical young dupe – he had taken the trouble to count how many people were executed in connection with one piece of information that they *might* have learned.

3823 dead then.

It's really unnecessary this time. I'll speak to Three, and have him try to persuade that . . .

He stopped. The epithet that quivered on the edge of his mind was so obscene, it shocked him. Consciously, then, he cautioned himself: 'Establishing a new order requires hard actions. People are incorrigible in these early stages, and easily revert to old-style behaviour. The world still swarms with counter-revolutionaries, wreckers, right and left deviationists, opportunists –'

The glib phrases by which the regime labelled its potential enemies ran their courses through his mind, as he went out into the corridor, and down a palace elevator, and along another vast hallway to Three's office.

He found Jodell in his office; and his entrance was a surprise; for the man looked up from a document he had been reading, and for a few moments he was blank.

Fourteen said, 'I'm beginning to think I misunderstood the instructions you gave me.'

'Instructions?' echoed Three.

'It is possible I should report to you on the case I was assigned.'

Suddenly, then, blankness ended.

The older man rose hastily. 'No, no,' he said sharply, 'Not one word. This is between you and The Leader.'

'It's really quite simple,' the other went on. 'I –'

'*Stop it!*' screeched Number Three. He put his hands over his ears. 'Are you out of your mind? Not another word from you.'

The reaction was fantastic now. The man's eyes were wild, his face twisted; he kept trying to control himself, but it was a hideous failure.

Williams backed away. 'Okay, okay,' he said, 'you've convinced me. I gather that there are no intermediate channels on this, and I promise you it will not happen again.'

'It had better not,' was the grim reply. 'Now, go to your quarters, and wait there until you are called.'

Williams, though he did not have a military background, nevertheless drew himself up at this point, and saluted. 'Very well, sir. I guarantee no more laxness. May I leave your presence?'

'Yes, go.'

The young man departed; and though his outward manner was calm, inwardly he was shaking.

To him had come the most terrible realization – I have a memory, a piece of information, which must be disposed of.

What he knew was absolutely basic.

For a few minutes, nearly a year ago now, Higenroth had shown a power that transcended the regime. For those minutes the entire world was bright with images that derived from one old man's genius.

Basic information . . .

Fourteen walked along the gleaming marble. All around him were the accoutrements of power and wealth: great stairways, high ceilings, massive chandeliers. How great he had felt, he remembered, when he had first been invited to this centre of the universe.

Thinking of that, he was only vaguely aware of the troop of uniformed men who emerged from a side corridor and came toward him. His vagueness ended abruptly, as he realized that they had stopped and were barring his way. He stopped, also.

'Sir, are you Crother Williams?' The speaker was a youth in a captain's uniform.

Williams acknowledged his identity after the tiniest hesitation. Once he had been as young and assured as this youthful officer with his bright brown eyes and his pink face.

'I have instructions,' said the youth, 'to escort you to a certain place.'

Williams did not ask where that place was. He nodded and fell into step behind the captain; was aware of the half-dozen youths with rifles walking behind him. The little procession came presently to a large, open door with a high arch. Through this door and arch they went and into a courtyard he did not recall ever having seen before. It was a high-walled area about thirty feet by forty, with not a shrub or a bunch of grass visible in or around its concrete flatness.

The young captain pointed at one of the walls. 'Stand over there,' he said.

Williams walked over slowly, and as slowly turned around. He saw that the six men had formed into a line, facing him; and that the youth had taken out a document. He glanced down at it, and said, 'I have an order here for your execution.'

Williams backed toward the wall until he felt its hardness against his shoulders. As he stood there, he was aware of the officer reading out the charges, as required by law:

'Serious errors ... Poor leadership ... Unclear and indecisive stand ... Diversionary acts ...'

The young man folded the paper, and placed it in his pocket. Up came his chin. On his face a stern expression.

'Is that it?' asked Williams.

'That's it.'

It's amazing, thought the former member of the Supreme Praesidium of Earth, who had until a few minutes ago been the fourteenth most powerful person on the planet, that is exactly a correct evaluation of what I did, in terms of Lilgin's reality ...

In the nine years since his appointment he had grown from a youthful dupe through the role of apologist, through – further – attempts to make amends, through – additional – a new attempt at rationalization. But now, finally, he stood before the firing squad, silent.

He presumed he would be allowed to say last words. But there was nothing to say, and indeed no one to say it to. Who among the other desperates – the superior survival types – would want to hear what a failure had said? Who of them, in fact, would even want it known that he had some interest in the last statement of Crother Williams?

Williams thought: because of that man – Lilgin – I had not one moment of truth in me. I lived not one second as a thinking person where I was not twisted; since childhood I have striven to fit into his crooked frame.

Not one second.

When the bullets hit him, he actually lay down and curled into a semblance of the prenatal position ... Not one second, he thought, lying there.

Or at least it seemed as if he thought it.

SEVEN

'Some day,' said Ishkrin, with a smile, 'we will discover why during the past eighteen years the best communication scientists in the world have had this small city built for them next to the palace, and why we live here like kings . . . except for one little thing.'

He was a man with a large moustache, about fifty years old. Until his speech he had been sitting silently eating his lunch, with only occasional darting glances at his dozen or so luncheon companions.

No one spoke immediately. Then:

'What's the one exception?' asked the new man from across the table. He was a handsome youth who had been introduced to Ishkrin and the others that morning. His name was Orlo Thomas. His seat at the table was number one, south.

To ask his question Orlo had looked up. In doing so, he grew aware that all the men at the table had stopped eating and were watching him, grinning. Despite their reaction, he still did not realize that Ishkrin's remark had actually been made for his benefit.

'To get out,' explained Ishkrin, who was a small man and in fact with his moustache and shaggy hair looked a bit like Martin Lilgin, the dictator, 'we have to go through the palace –'

'So? –'

'That's not permitted.'

'How do you mean?' The first faint shock of realization was now reflected in Orlo's eyes. Simultaneously, his young brows knit into a puzzled frown. 'I came in that way.'

With the perversity of the inured, the older men watched him with even wider grins, as the deadly reality was driven home.

'It's not permitted,' Ishkrin repeated.

For a long moment, Orlo sat there. The emotions that now flitted across his face had altered. Perhaps these new colleagues wanted to find out how he could take a joke; that was what his expression suddenly telegraphed.

He laughed uncertainly. Then, abruptly, he pushed away his plate, with its lunch only partly eaten. In the same unceremonious fashion he shoved his chair away from the table and jumped energetically to his feet, and, without another word, hurried along, past six dozen other tables in the glitteringly beautiful commissary to the distant exit door.

After he had gone, the only sound at his table was the somewhat deafening conversation that drifted over from the other tables. The men leaned back in their chairs. No one ate. Almost every eye twinkled expectantly.

Finally, a slim little man who occupied seat number seven, east, who was a mathematical specialist, and whose name was Anden Duryea, said, 'We have just witnessed the power of a single thought, when presented with a certain significance, to stimulate a human being to swift action. He's gone to check. It may be that, being young and brash, he may even attempt to leave Communications City.'

Another man, Peter Rosten - seat three, south - shook his head after a moment. 'I respect your analysis, sir, as far as it goes,' he commented in a patient voice. 'But I urgently suggest that what we have just witnessed is not nly the power of one thought. It is a unique event as well.' He was a medium-tall individual with strong, sturdy-looking shoulders. His category was electronics. He sent his grey gaze questioningly around the table, 'How many of you,' he asked, 'when you were told that you were probably a prisoner, headed for the palace to see if you could get out?'

Nobody had. And that held them, and startled them, for a minute or more. 'Amazing.' 'It's true.' 'I accepted the fact without argument.' 'What I did was wait for an apartment to be assigned to me, and sure enough the assignment came through by mid-afternoon.' 'When I got to my apartment, and saw how relatively sumptuous it was, I was briefly lulled. But even then I didn't test.'

'Perhaps,' Rosten continued in that same, deep, patient voice, 'the regime really does love the young, or wants to, but forgets once in a while. What could be our new, young associate's crime?'

Ishkrin, who had been listening with a faint smile, said, 'And now, Peter, I regret that I must correct you. In Lilgin land there are no crimes; there are only charges. The question is, what are the charges against him?'

Rosten bowed his large head. 'I stand corrected. In retrospect the word I used almost seems like an attempt at conciliation.'

A lean man who had not hitherto spoken – seat nine, north – whose name was Sandy McIntosh, an engineer who was freckled and had reddish rather than sandy hair, said earnestly, 'As we older men learned, it's not the few like our new associate that matter – single individuals can be invalidated, their reputations ruined by mere accusations. What counts is the great mass of the ever young, who don't know anything and don't remember the facts – because they never knew them. They're the ones that are supposed to be treated like pure bunnies by the regime. But it forgets all too often, and treats them badly, too.' He shook his fifty-ish head. 'That man is so villainous, so suspicious, he can't help himself. He has to strike and strike, and kill and kill. Amazing. Yet, as we observe it, we presume that he also was once a baby, once a boy, a youth, a young man, and that there was a time when he had feelings.'

'That was before he got the ideal,' said a tall, gaunt man – seat fifteen, west – whose category was also in a branch of physics: electro-magnetic phenomena. His name was Dan Matt.

'The truth we must observe here,' said Peter Rosten, shrugging those thick shoulders, 'is that singlehandedly he is creating a new civilization in spite of all of us. Almost, so to speak, he is doing it over the dead bodies of three billion people.'

'I doubt if he's killed more than a billion,' Ishkrin said in his correcting tone. 'Let's not have any unscientific estimates in a scientific centre like this.' He broke off, 'Ssshh, here comes our young man.'

It was a slow progress they witnessed. The youth was dragging his feet. His head was down. He seemed to be in deep thought.

During his journey back to the table, no one ate anything. They simply sat and watched him, as if they had endless time. Which was, in its sad way, true. For they had lived here now in this modern, up-to-date centre year after year with only an occasional work assignment.

They had all brightened a little at the coming of the new man; though he was absurdly young to be here in a scientific centre. The estimates of his age ranged from eighteen to twenty. They couldn't imagine it being *less* than the smaller number; and his pink, youthful face was as beautiful as a young girl's. As a girl they would have put him at sixteen or seventeen. But for a male, twenty: no more.

What was exciting about a new arrival was that he always brought new information. And so the old-timers picked up his special knowledge and added it to their own training and experience. After which the entire group reverted to its perennial state of intellectual somnolence – and good humour.

Orlo sank into the seat he had vacated about ten minutes earlier, looked around at the grinning faces, and shook his head, wonderingly. 'Gentlemen,' he said, 'would you like to know what happened?'

Instantly, several protesting voices resisted the offer of information, and said in effect, 'Spare us the unnecessary details.' But these few were quickly overwhelmed by a majority approval. Ishkrin spoke for the larger group, 'As was pointed out, our young friend did a unique thing. So we should know. How did the guards at the door handle it? What did they say?'

The youth said simply, 'I walked toward them, and walked through the door without talking to anyone. They didn't expect that. So I was thirty feet into the palace before I was overtaken by an officer and two soldiers, and firmly, forcibly led back.'

'But what did they say?' asked Peter Rosten.

Orlo smiled. He seemed to be recovering from his earlier shock; was more into the timeless spirit of these older men; more acceptant of their purely intellectual interest in all of the fine points of a dictatorial system. His voice actually enjoyed itself as he said, 'The officer on duty told me, "Sir, you have to have an authorization to go into the palace." I said, "Captain, I'm not trying to go into the palace. I want to go out to the street." He said, "You can't go out by way of the palace." Then I said, "All right, show me the other way out." He said, "There is no other way out." I said, "Then you mean I'm a prisoner here?" "No, but you need an authorization to get out." "All right, take me to the person from whom I can obtain such an authorization." "From Chairman Lilgin only." "Very well, send Chairman Lilgin my respectful request for such an authorization." "I'm sorry, I'm not authorized to communicate with his excellency." "Who is? Is anyone here authorized?" "Nobody here." "Then I'm a prisoner?" "No, all you need is Chairman Lilgin's authorization." "Does he never come into this section?" "No." "Then I'm a prisoner?" "No, but I must ask you to leave this entranceway. You are obstructing this passageway."

'There were a few more remarks,' Orlo concluded, 'but I finally came back here, as you see.'

Silence. Finally, the overweight man in seat thirteen, west – Samuel Ober, colour photography and electronics – said, 'The logic of the guard officer's position is unchallengeable. You are not a prisoner in law. You are a prisoner only within the frame of his authorization. Like a computer that is not programmed to include you in its calculations, he cannot deal with you at all.'

Orlo was suddenly quite cheerful. 'What happens next?'

'You will be assigned an apartment.' The speaker was a big man, black as coal – seat number five, east, name: Gar Yuyu; electro-magnetic phenomena, biological section – 'usually,' he added, 'this is done between three and three-thirty in the afternoon.'

The great Ishkrin moustache jiggled. 'What are the charges against you?' he asked from his twelve north seat.

The youth smiled an unusually grim smile. 'No charges against me. I was simply told that I am being promoted.'

The men looked blank. Once again eating ceased. 'But that's impossible.' 'There have to be charges.' 'What you're saying is unheard of.'

There was more, but some of the sentences got lost in the general clamour. Finally, silence settled again; and Peter Rosten said, 'Promoted to what?'

'I haven't been told what this one is. But I previously refused a promotion to take over my boss's job on the east coast.'

'Oh.' Duryea uttered the exclamation. 'Now, the picture clarifies.' The slim little mathematician nodded as if the matter were indeed explained. 'People do not refuse promotions on Lilgin's earth.'

'I refused,' said Orlo.

'Then you were charged accordingly.'

'No. I said I did not believe myself to be as qualified as the person occupying the position. They said let them be the judge. And I said, no, for the good of the people I refused to take over from a more competent person.'

'At least,' smiled Ishkrin, 'you know the jargon.'

'What happened next?' asked Duryea.

'I continued with my previous duties until, yesterday afternoon, I was released from my tasks and told to report here this morning, and that I would be offered another promotion. I asked, to what? The person in personnel who gave me my instructions didn't know. I said that I reserved the right to refuse this new promotion, also. He said that was up to me.'

'And this is where he sent you?' persisted Duryea.

'Yes.'

'Then you've been charged.'

'No,' said Orlo, with a smile – he looked as if he was beginning to enjoy the intricate argument – 'that wouldn't be legal.' He added, 'It is generally agreed even among Lilgin's severest critics that no one has ever been deprived of anything without charges first being placed against him. What you're implying is that charges exist which have not yet been made to me publicly, and that would be illegal.'

'But –' protested a man who had not hitherto spoken – six, east, a Chinese astronomer, with the occidentalized name Jimmy Ho – 'everybody is here in this centre for something. Even I had charges placed against me seventeen years ago, and I've been here ever since.'

'No, I am here for nothing,' said Orlo. He had been leaning back in his chair, breathing deeply, totally involved in the interchange. Now, with an abrupt movement he stood up, and sent his gaze around the table as if he were a lecturer and they his audience. 'Gentlemen,' he said, 'it is beginning to be obvious that you fit the typical Lilgin-land stereotype of persons who have been placed in a restricted category, and I don't. In short, you all should be in this place. But that does not apply to me.'

The first reaction of his listeners was to smile as if they were amused by the conceit of his attitude. Years of their peculiar imprisonment had brought a calm based on a philosophy which, though it differed from individual to individual, had in its inner meaning several common denominators. First, they could not be insulted. Second, their response to what looked like an attack was to assume that it was part of the attacker's own good humour.

So, now, they waited expectantly for one of their number to come up with a suitable – meaning equally one-up – reply. When after a minute not a single person had spoken (and Orlo continued to stand there, smiling, and as if waiting), it was Ishkrin who said in amazement, 'Come to think of it, the insult is total. Nobody has ever told us that we belong here. Now, think. Isn't that true?'

'Well, I'll be damned.' 'Yes, you're right, this is the first time.' 'We may joke, but we all feel put upon.'

As they uttered these reactions, the youth stood at his place at the table, and gazed at them with bright, blue eyes and the smile of enjoyment. When silence finally descended, he said, 'May I enlarge on my criticism?'

The mathematician, Duryea, sighed. 'We might as well learn his philosophy in one lump, instead of getting it piecemeal over the years.' He nodded at Orlo. 'Yes, speak. Tell all.'

Most of the others nodded, also. And Peter Rosten said almost pleasantly in that normally calm voice, 'Somehow, right now a human thought seems more important than usual. So he's already done that for us.'

Orlo said, 'I am now going to deliver a brief speech.' Which he proceeded to do: 'Gentlemen, there will come a time in human evolution when this little game of a dictator catching the young and using them, will no longer work. Your failure was that when you were young you were made use of and you didn't notice it. You happily took over top positions from older men of that day, and didn't observe that their demotion was part of an endless system whereby one man used unknowing young people for his own purposes. Suddenly, you were too old and too smart for the system, but it was too late. You had played your part as a dupe, and the next crop of unaware youth was already sufficiently educated to take over from you.

'My role and my fate –' Orlo shrugged – '*I* had figured this out by the time I was fifteen. So a week ago when I was notified that I was to take over a key position from a man of 32, I rejected the promotion, as I've already told you. I immediately told everybody that I knew, of my own age, and sent letters by the hundreds to other late-teens, explaining why I had done it. Most of them are untraceable, I feel sure, because at the time I was not suspected. The final few, I presume, were not delivered, but by then I had spread my poison. What do you think? Will even one of those youthful recipients silently pick up the torch, and carry on?'

He sat down as abruptly as he had got up earlier. But the controversy went on beyond the lunch hour. The consensus was in the negative.

'It's too few,' said the mathematician, Duryea. 'Remember, this man kills everybody who is dangerous to him. Not just ringleaders, but everyone who has certain thoughts or memories in his head.' He seemed struck by his own analysis. 'At least,' he said, 'the power of human thought has been given ultimate recognition. Specific ideas, no matter whose heads they are in, are assigned a death sentence status. Those persons no matter how numerous must be destroyed who have those thoughts.'

'You have them,' argued Orlo, 'and you remain alive. I have them, and I have not yet even been charged, let alone killed.'

Immediately, the older man was in good humour again. 'We're a special group here,' said Duryea. 'We're scientifically up to date communications experts. From time to time we are given problems to solve, but for the most part we just sit here wasting our talents. The ultimate judgement has been rendered on scientific research. It has no value except in relation to the needs of one man. So the question is –' He paused.

Ishkrin said with his crinkle of a smile, 'Yes, yes, Anden, what is the question?'

Duryea climbed to his feet. Seen erect, he was even smaller than he had appeared sitting down. His face and manner had the look of someone who has been startled by a sudden insight. His eyes gleaming excitedly, he said urgently, 'Gentlemen, we *are* here for a purpose. Those previous tasks were red herrings, designed to confuse us, so that when the real problem was presented we'd think of it as being on the same level.' In his agitation, he swung about and faced seat number three south. 'Peter,' he said, 'tell them what you mentioned to me earlier.'

He finished breathlessly, 'The real problem was the one that came in this morning. Peter – tell them!'

Peter Rosten of the voice that never seemed to get excited found himself in one instant the focus of everybody's attention. He had an edge on these boon companions in that General Stul Armidge, administrator for the 'city' had known him as a young man, and still didn't hesitate to pick up the phone and call old Peter and chat with him about this and that. During such a phone call that morning, the general had casually mentioned the new project.

'Remember Higenroth –' Peter began.

Just about everybody groaned; cut him off. 'Oh, no,' somebody said then. 'For God's sake,' said another, 'not the Pervasive Theory.' Still others: 'I thought Glucken was given the job of solving that.' 'Now, we're going to have problems.' 'As if we didn't have enough to worry about just sitting here –'

'Gentlemen, calm yourselves,' said Peter Rosten. 'You have six months to rediscover the system. Plenty of time, surely.'

Orlo Thomas had been glancing from face to face. During a moment of silence, he said, 'Pervasive *what*?'

Sandy McIntosh moaned, 'That's all we need. Someone who's never even heard of it.' He waved a freckled hand at the youth. 'Don't worry, kid, you'll hear enough in due time.'

A plump man, Number Twelve West, climbed to his feet. 'Well, I think I'll be going to the library and begin briefing myself on Pervasive Theory, and start thinking. If that's our problem, we'd better be prepared to deliver. Or we may find ourselves no longer treated like kings.'

He walked off without a backward glance. His departure evoked a variety of responses from his colleagues.

A hitherto silent man – seat ten, north – rolled a pair of expressive brown eyes ceiling-ward, and said, 'Kings – to be locked up in here for eight years, like I've been – it feels like slavery.'

'What are you complaining about?' demanded Ishkrin. 'The story is that Lilgin hasn't left the palace in over twenty years.'

'Bui he *could* if he wanted to.'

'Why don't you just tell yourself that you could, also?'

'But it wouldn't be true.'

Ishkrin threw up his hands. He said to Orlo, 'You see the kind of people we have here. What's good enough for the dictator of the world is not good enough for them. People are really incorrigible.'

Their table companions had been getting up from their places, and with a variety of leave-taking remarks, were wandering away. In the end only Ishkrin and Orlo remained. The former glanced at his watch, and then said to the youth in a kindly voice, 'I'd advise you to go to the assembly room and wait there until you are assigned your own apartment.'

Orlo leaned back in his chair. A faint frown creased that beautiful boyish face. 'I'm trying to fit my presence here into a logical frame. And I can't do it. Can you?'

'I hadn't thought about it,' the older man replied.

'Nor I – until I listened to you and the others.'

'Do you have scientific training?'

'Of a sort.'

'What does that mean?'

'Well –' a wan smile – 'I'm a sort of systems engineer.'

'Why do you say, sort of?'

'I was never allowed to finish any portion of my training. I was, so to speak, dipped into every science except – please notice the significance of the omission – except communications.' Orlo shook his head. 'So, for God's sake, what am I doing here?'

'That is odd.' Ishkrin crinkled that mighty, bushy moustache, then: 'Well, we mustn't assume irrationality. In its own fashion everything in Lilgin land follows a total rationale, though the reality is not always easy to see. Let me think about it, also.' He stood up, short and stocky. 'It's now 3.15 P.M. So you'd better get over to where the administrative office can find you easily. I'll take you over to the assembly room if you wish.'

'It's not necessary. I found it in my morning wanderings.' Orlo stood up. 'After my overnight flight, I got here early and I've looked the city – is that what you gentlemen call it? – over. If this is my future home, I already know where the main locations are.

'But,' he concluded, frowning again, 'even my staying

here doesn't seem logical. In fact, I'll be surprised if I'm actually assigned a room.'

By four o'clock he still hadn't been. And for some reason that bothered him in a way that, being young, he didn't notice right away.

EIGHT

At one minute to six o'clock, when Orlo reported to administration on the first floor for the third time, he found the last employee, a girl, was on the verge of locking up. She had her coat on, and was obviously about to leave.

'I'm sorry,' she said, 'I have no room assignment for you. Perhaps, in the morning –'

'But – tonight?' Orlo protested. 'Where do I stay tonight?'

'I'm sorry.' She was in a hurry now, a dark-haired young woman with a large bosom and matching plump face but with an attractive figure. 'You mustn't try to make this my problem,' she said firmly. 'Step aside, please.'

Orlo backed slowly to the door, and now for the first time he braced himself. With each retreating step, he could feel himself recovering from the peculiar concern that had been developing in him . . . Of course, he thought, it isn't her problem. In fact, why regard it as a problem? –

He smiled at the girl as she passed him in the hall. 'I won't make any further inquiries,' he said. 'I'll sleep on the floor, somewhere. Regard that as permanently settled.'

She paused, at those words. Seemed to be slightly disturbed for him. Then hastily, 'I have to be out of this part of the building by 6:15 P.M. After that there is no authorization for anyone at all to make their exit from here through the palace.'

'I understana the perfect logic involved,' said Orlo with amused calm.

The young woman seemed not to hear. She was walking rapidly again. And she did not pause as, half-turning her head, she flung another statement at him: 'I mention this because the one night that I was slow I found a couch in a sitting room at the end of corridor H.'

Orlo called with a smile, 'Next time you get left behind, I'll join you there.'

'Goodbye!' screamed the girl. 'My name is Lidla.'

She turned a corner, and was gone.

Orlo walked slowly in the same direction as she had gone. He was at inner peace now except for a slight amazement with himself. It was unfortunate that he had allowed the neglect about the room to upset him. He must make sure that he never again let anything that happened either depress or elate him.

I must smile as I look at those S.O.B.s in the palace, and smile as I watch my unfortunate colleagues here. I cannot let them be my problem. And I cannot be a problem to myself, ever.

The thought ended, for he had come to a cross corridor. And there, walking toward him was Ishkrin. The little man with the blond moustache that spread like a walrus's nose hair across his cheerful face, waved at him.

'Did they find you?' he asked.

'Who?'

'The officer of the guard and three of his men.'

Orlo suppressed a tiny chill by a quick recollection of his just-decided-on defensive thought. 'Did they say what they wanted?' he asked, calm again, and without problems.

'They wanted you.' Ishkrin's eyes were bright.

'If they're sincere,' said Orlo comfortably, 'they'll no doubt locate me presently.'

He started to walk past, but Ishkrin put one hand on his arm, and restrained him. 'You have no idea what this could be?' he asked in a low voice.

'Perhaps,' the youth replied airily, 'they wish to inform me of my apartment assignment.'

'That's never been done by the guard before. In fact –' he made a significant gesture, and they started walking '– the guard coming in here and searching for someone is itself a unique event.'

'Oh – very good,' was the best reply Orlo could muster, 'then we may all learn something new. So long.'

This time Ishkrin made no attempt to hold him. As Orlo turned into a side corridor, the older man called, 'Dinner for us Science Kings is at seven, in case you're still around.'

Orlo waved, but did not look back.

The science 'city', through which he had been moving and through which he continued to stroll, was the most fantastic constructed thing that he had seen in his twenty years. Being of course of a somewhat perverse nature – otherwise he wouldn't have done the deliberate actions that had brought him to this strange prison – he had until this moment not really been able to put his attention on the fabulous surroundings. Treated them much as some people treat museums, giving them the glancing look and the swift passage through.

Now, he did the opposite . . . I am, he thought, trying to make up my mind, so I'll slow down – He did. And he looked closely at what there was to see. What he saw was not exactly incredible; it merely seemed that way.

Each corridor was about forty feet wide and fifty high. The marble walls were decorated with metallic shapes and metallic writing. Those gleaming shapes and words seemed to tell an intricate story. As far as he could make out, here was the complete account of scientific communication on earth. Every device used, every circuit ever conceived by a human mind, the theory in diagrams, the inventors in bold relief, everything about its development told in little printed stories and in mathematical formulae.

The particular hallway he was in was, of course, only one facet of the history and the science. Now that he was looking, he found himself remembering fragments of what he had glanced at in his wanderings that morning. Of course, not knowing the facts he could only presume that they were all here. But the purpose, as it had been explained to him by his then guide, was to provide the experts with continual stimulation. Thus – the hope went – they would presently see new relationships. And inventions would blossom hour by hour.

His own attention wandered suddenly . . . Two ways, thought Orlo, to react to a search if you are the object: evade, was one. Find the seeker, was the other. (What you did with him when you had located him was of course dependent on the circumstances.)

A man being searched for reflected, in a sense, the relationship of life with death; thus Orlo argued speciously with himself, mildly amused. Life was essentially a curve up from the cradle and then down into the grave. In the up-stage of that curve, one almost didn't notice the man with the scythe. But in the down stage – ah, there was the analogy in beautiful synchronization. Almost in the same way as a man being searched for hid from his searchers, so during the down-curve of life people sought to conceal themselves in doctors' offices, hospitals, rest homes, and in health food and drug stores.

On the other hand, bold men were known to have walked up to Death, and by looking him squarely in the eye, occasionally cowed him, and sent him slinking back to his lair. And so, having routed the Evil Old Man, they sometimes survived for an unusually long time.

That one, decided Orlo the Bold.

Accordingly, a few minutes later he approached the huge, brilliantly lighted entrance to the corridor that connected the dictator's palace and the Communications City. He sauntered up to where an assistant Officer of the Guard sat behind one of those high desks. He did not fail to note that standing at attention on either side of the guardroom door were six uniformed men with rifles. He said, 'Lieutenant, my name is Orlo Thomas –'

That was as far as he got. Electrifying reaction. The youthful officer snatched at his desk top intercom, and said into it urgently, 'Captain, Mr. Thomas has just arrived at the desk.'

'Be there on the double –' The baritone voice came out of the speaker with the natural sound of the Higenrothian zero system, just as if the man who spoke was standing there in front of them.

A pause. Then, an astonishing thing. Orlo had turned casually, expecting that the little group of uniformed searchers would presently emerge from the communications centre by way of one of several corridors. Five of the huge hallways emptied into the foyer.

Out of the middle one, a rapid movement. The next instant, an officer with captain's insignia burst forth at a dead run. Trailing behind him, but doing their best to keep up, came three sergeants.

The four made it to the desk within seconds of each other. All seemed equally breathless, but the captain spoke at once: 'Mr. Thomas . . . puff-puff . . . you will . . . puff-puff . . . accompany me . . . puff-puff . . . into the palace – This way, sir!'

Orlo strolled through the door, and was conscious of the four hard-breathing men behind him. A moment later, the captain who had evidently recovered sufficiently, darted in front of Orlo, and said, 'I hope you don't mind a brisker pace.'

He didn't wait for a reply. His pace quickened to a stride, then to a lope. 'Hope you don't mind, sir,' he gasped.

'Where are we going?' By this time Orlo was gasping, himself.

'You have been invited to attend a special dinner, sir. And they're waiting.'

'Invited – by whom? Puff-puff.'

Even as he breathed the question hoarsely, Orlo had an improbable thought. At once, he chided himself. Because it was absolutely ridiculous.

'His excellency, Martin Lilgin,' gulped the youthful captain. Even in its breathlessness, his voice had awe in it. And something of the disbelief that Orlo himself was feeling.

Nothing more was said. The five of them charged forward. Ahead, the lights grew brighter. The corridor widened. Abruptly, they came to what had already been visible: a cross corridor of the same imposing size. Into this they turned, slowing.

Orlo noticed the sudden hold-back of the captain, and braced himself down to a walk. Amazingly, just in time. Within a yard or two only around the corner, was a barrier. A long gleaming fence, and behind it a desk. On the other side of the desk sat a dozen uniformed men with grim faces. They were all extremely young men, like his escorts. One of them – an individual who was surely not more than twenty-two or -three – wore general's insignia.

Of the eleven other young men, Orlo observed in a single glance, three were colonels, and the rest lieutenant-colonels and majors. He was a counter, and he took the time to do exactly that. The latter two ranks were evenly divided: four each.

Even as he made his rapid observations, his young captain-escort strode up to the fence beyond which the general and his staff sat. He saluted smartly, and reported in a formal tone, 'Captain Ruthers, escorting Mr. Orlo Thomas.'

The young general stood up, and so did the entire line-up of officers. But only the general returned the salute. During these rituals, his frown did not soften, nor did the frowns of his subordinates. But it was his steel grey eyes that fixed on Orlo.

'Mr. Thomas, will you do us the courtesy of stepping over here to the Com-identi at the gate?'

Orlo stepped over with the automatic reaction of all good citizens of Lilgin-land, who had been confronted by such machines many thousands of times. Silently, he thrust his hand up to and including the wrist into an opening in the device. There was a buzzing sound; presumably, the distant computer was comparing whatever it was in his fingers, hand, or wrist, that it looked at with a facsimile in its memory code. And, of course, as always it swiftly recognized that, yes, here indeed was the individual it had known for almost twenty years as Orlo Thomas.

A green light blinked on. Whereupon, the youthful officer with the super-rank gestured toward a man down the line. 'Major Clukes, open the gate!'

At this command, a youth of no more than Orlo's years turned and walked with stiff military precision to the gate, bent forward, did something with his fingers; at which the gate unlatched and swung open.

'Enter, Mr. Thomas,' said the general.

Orlo, suppressing an impulse to walk stiffly, moved forward and through. The major closed the gate behind him. And at that moment Orlo realized something. His own attention had been so fixated by the impressive military manoeuvre at the desk and the gate that he had been only dimly conscious of what was beyond: a high wall with golden doors.

Two doors. Tall. Wide. Glistening. Closed.

At once, he realized that he had also been aware of something else.

From beyond the doors came a sound of men laughing, and shouting, and singing. It seemed impossible. It was muffled. But it was – now that he was able to give it attention – unmistakable. Wild laughter. Actual shouts. Raucous singing.

Good God!

He was so intent, and baffled, that it took several moments for him to realize that the drama behind him was not completed. With that, he turned, blinking a little.

What he saw was that Captain Ruthers had presented a paper. 'May I have your signature, sir?' he asked. 'Testifying, Mr. Orlo Thomas safely delivered into your keeping.'

The grim-faced general accepted the document, signed it, stamped it, and handed it back. 'That will be all, Captain,' he said curtly.

A military style withdrawal now occurred: Salute. Back-up of several steps. Formal turn. The sergeants falling in step. And the march off down the hall of the captain and his non-coms.

'This way, Mr. Thomas –' The general's voice jarred Orlo from his somewhat wide-eyed interest in those precision proceedings.

Orlo turned, feeling rueful. He was, it seemed to him, being snapped from one episode of hypnotic absorption to another.

'This way,' turned out to be rather obvious: toward the big doors. But – Orlo was a little surprised – only the general of that array of a dozen was his escort. Equally startling, the officer actually opened the door without knocking.

Before Orlo could think about the implications of that, the uproar from inside, and the first visual impact of what was there hit him.

NINE

There are moments in almost everyone's life that are, somehow, impressed as vividly on the mind as a good picture on a photographic print. There, forever captured by the camera of the brain, a scene remains etched in brilliant colour. And is always available thereafter to be looked at again, and re-examined in minute detail.

This was such a scene.

What Orlo saw was a small room, comparatively, in terms of width and length. Though of course it was the same fifty feet high as the corridor.

In that room was, on one side, a table set for about thirty people. The other side was floor space.

That's where the thirty people were.

Not all of the thirty were yelling, nor singing, nor laughing. At least, not all of them at the same time. But enough were doing one or the other simultaneously to create bedlam.

For moments and moments and moments the sheer improbability of what he was seeing held Orlo blank. And kept him standing there. Belatedly, he saw that each of that small group – and surely two and a half dozen was a small source for such an uproar . . . held a glass with, mostly, coloured liquid in it. At once, understanding.

These men were drunk.

And they were men only. Not a single woman in view. The vaunted equalizing of male and female, so forcefully promoted in all the lower reaches of the society, had no place in this room.

Drunk! Here, at the heart of earth power, where surely minds should be clear hour after day after year, the members of the Supreme Praesidium of an entire planet – plastered.

He recognized famous faces: Megara, Jodell, Budoon, Kahler, Peterson, Roquet, Fafard – the inner council people. One or other of those super seven was always making some weighty statement on television. What they said all minor executives had better know, because as of that minute it was the party line.

There were other familiar faces in that throng. But they were a step or two down from the seven. For them, in Orlo's memory, it was a step into anonymity. That lean fellow with the aquiline nose, one of the singers: Sosatin? And the heavy-set man with the square jaw: Domalo? And – he fumbled even more uncertainly with one of the other names: Cas . . . Cas . . . what? Whatever his name, he was arguing in a shrieking voice with a man who yelled back in a thick voice absolutely fogged over by intoxication.

The general was tugging at his sleeve. 'This way, Mr. Thomas.'

Orlo shuffled into the room, automatically moved forward by the words. He had never imagined a moment like this; so he couldn't really walk normally. In all the thoughts he had ever had, which included intensely critical, even murderous feelings, he at whom those mental missiles were directed was, in those days, far away. He was a remote, hateful being whose scheming and bestialness the then teen Orlo believed himself to have exposed (to himself) with the sharp, cutting blow of reason.

And now, after mere minutes of warning, here he was approaching an impossible meeting with that incredible rat, that mass murderer, that greatest plotter of all time against the human race.... Will he be curt? Discourteous? Accusing? Will he strike at me contemptuously with the back of his hand? (And I have to stand there and take it, for fear of being instantly murdered.) Will he speak to me at all, or just nod and turn away, indifferently?

It was too much too soon. Earlier, at the time of bracing himself to spend the night sleeping on a floor, he had thought that nothing could shake him again. But he was shaken now. His mind kept scattering, his walk as unsteady as that of any of the drunks in the room.

Staggering, Orlo followed the general through that gesticulating throng. The two men veered past the raucous group of singers, the bobbing uniform in front, Orlo weaving along in the rear. They followed a pathway that took them around out-bent elbows and gesturing liquor glasses, past the big heads of two small men, and up to a third, normal-sized head atop the slender body of another small man.

This third little fellow had a moustache with the same walrus spread as equally little Ishkrin. There was a difference, however. In fact, several differences. Ishkrin's moustache had a lot of grey intermixed with its brown. This one was black. Ishkrin's face, as much of it as was visible, had the crinkles and wrinkles of honourable ageing. Lilgin's face was smoother. His was the skin of a man of thirty-eight or so. Which, of course, was impossible.

Orlo had no time to consider how impossible, or why. He was noticing that the dictator was dressed like a dandy.

For some reason, that surprised him. There were other surprises. He had not expected the great man to be so small.

So that's why he hasn't left the palace in twenty years . . .

The man's elegance was even more unexpected. He was dapper. He wore a tan suit of radical cut, but spotless, and perfectly fitted.

Black hair, black moustache, young, firm face . . .

He was beautiful.

The greatest surprise of all: this perfect little person gave him a smile of greeting and a handshake, and said in his famous baritone voice, that absolutely masculine vibrance: 'And here we have, I believe, the only young man on the planet who has ever turned down a top classification promotion. Special things like that are reported to me, young man. We must have a chat about it. That's for later, of course. Right now . . .'

He released Orlo's palm, and clapped his hands.

Thunder.

For God's sake, thought Orlo, he's got some kind of negative and positive connectors in his palms. And, when he claps, the sound is amplified from the ceiling . . .

The consequences were lightning fast. Singing ceased. Yellers stopped arguing at the top of their voices. Screaming laughter choked into silence. In a flash the drunks transformed into a normal group of dinner guests heading for the table.

To Orlo, the little man said, 'Sit in the red chair directly across from me.'

He pointed. He pushed ever so slightly at Orlo's arm, who felt impelled to walk around the table to the indicated chair. He stood behind it, then, waiting as for a signal. He stood there precisely because everyone else was also standing. And waiting too.

Then the little man sat down. And that was evidently the signal. For there was a sudden sound of chairs dragging on the floor, and the breathing of men sitting down. And other noises. Also, the talking which had momentarily ended began again.

At this point, Orlo made an intense inner effort to recover from the shock of what had happened so rapidly. Never quite made it. He did ask the man to his right to pass him something, and did ask the man to his left. 'Is the entire Praesidium present here this evening?' Incredibly, though he received an answer, he did not recall it seconds after hearing it.

In spite of the bravado that impelled him periodically to brace himself, Orlo permitted his gaze to stray occasionally to the famous figure at the head of the table . . . Why is it, he thought, some small men become Ishkrins – who presumably would not harm a bee – and others become Lilgins whose fingers are always squeezing the trigger of the killer gun?

For a while he strove, also, to follow the involved conversation that was going on around Lilgin – something about the big government farms, and a new policy about who should do the actual work. Lilgin seemed to be in favour of more automatic machinery, but an older man with a severe expression on his face (like a perpetual scowl) urged the importance of seeing to it that certain individuals – classified as D types – should always have to do manual labour.

'It's a matter of maintaining discipline, your excellency.'

'Perhaps you're right,' said Lilgin in a mild voice. 'But I have often thought we should try a system of more leisure. It's never been done, you know.'

The man with the scowl took the attitude that that might be all right for others, but it was not feasible for the D's.

Orlo ate slowly. And every bite carried with it the thought: what am I doing here? What happens next? What is this? It can't really be me sitting here at the table of the man I hate more than any other person in the world, listening to him being reasonable while the suck-ups demand repression. Presumably, Lilgin would finally allow himself to be overruled. (During the course of the meal, Orlo never actually heard him do so.)

Other thoughts poured: Suppose I'm suddenly ordered to be executed at the end of the meal? Commanded – as he graphically visualized it – to stand up against that wall . . . Where, if that happened, could he escape to?

He had already noticed that the dining room had four sets of doors: the big corridor entrance, through which he had been escorted into the place, and three sets of small, ordinary doors, each about seven feet high; no more. Waiters had used two of the doors for their rapid entrances and exits. His escape route, it seemed to Orlo, would have to be a choice between the kitchen entrances, on the one hand, and the unknown exit number four, on the other.

It was a wild speculation. But since there was, literally, no reason for him to be here at all, his mind kept fantasying about it. In his feverish imagining, he saw himself somehow breaking out of the dining room and fleeing into the depths of the palace. There, finally cornered by search parties, he would be remorselessly mowed down.

Orlo was in the process of feeling sad about his unhappy demise when – abruptly – the fourth door burst open, and a plump man came striding in.

Unexpected, incredible, fantastic . . .

The intruder was not well dressed. He wore red trousers and a purple tee shirt that was extra long. His face was round, and his eyes as brown as marbles.

'Hey, you people!' he said loudly, 'I'm here. Everybody come to attention!'

As those words were called out in a tone of superiority, and even insolence, the men at the table made a variety of small noticing movements – except for Lilgin, who did not turn, or look up, or cease eating.

The intruder half-ran, or at least strode rapidly, to the end of the table at Orlo's right. Pausing there, he raised an arm, pointed a finger dramatically at the dictator, and said arrogantly, 'Lilgin, what have you been up to that I should know about?'

Orlo was leaning back and staring at the man in blank disbelief. Then – still unbelieving – he glanced at the men at the table. After their initial stirrings, they seemed calm now, though perhaps slightly expectant. One man had a resigned *moue* on his face; but he was the only one.

Lilgin had finally, evidently, decided to recognize the situation. He sat quiet for a moment, and then said in an uncertain tone, 'Well –'

'Speak up,' commanded the newcomer. 'None of this mumbling into your moustache.'

'I was about to say, Krosco,' said Lilgin, 'that I'm probably guilty of something. But right now I don't know what. Do you have any suggestions?'

Orlo relaxed. Suddenly, he saw this as a staged affair. Lilgin's question was a come-on if he'd ever heard one.

'Come, come!' Krosco was demanding in a tone that brooked no nonsense, 'if you need to have your memory jogged, we'll bring in the necessary equipment –'

That must have struck somebody as funny, for there was a giggle from down the table somewhere.

Krosco ignored the interruption. 'What about the farm machinery for those D types?' He was scathing. 'You're not going to let those yes-men here fall all over themselves in their false belief that you like to dig it into people. You're not going to let them stop you from doing the right thing.'

'I must say,' said Lilgin, in a defensive tone, 'I am misunderstood. I'm a social engineer who means it, that's all.'

'Yes,' persisted Krosco, 'you're letting these vindictive types overrule your best judgement on the D types.'

'We're just talking yet,' said Lilgin. 'No decision has yet been made. Different points of view have been presented.'

'Well, then, who gets killed this time?' Krosco demanded. 'Anybody in this room going to get his? That's the main question –' For the first time he allowed his gaze to drift around the table. And his face broke into a smirk. 'You'll agree, gentlemen, that's what's important. Which of you rats gets his today? Or which rat somewhere?'

Orlo felt a chill. The words momentarily brought back his fantasy of himself being executed at the end of the meal. Nonetheless, since no one was looking at him, or at least didn't seem to be, he leaned toward the man to his right, and whispered, 'Who is Krosco?'

The man did not turn his head; but he moved his lips, and framed words that made a sufficient sound. 'The court jester,' he whispered.

After that, Orlo began to recover. He had only the dimmest recollection of what a court jester had been, historically. But what he saw here with his bright blue eyes, and brighter mind, was an incredible phenomenon. Krosco was the dictator's way of speaking aloud some of the real thoughts of the people present. The Fool, from time immemorial, had dared to say what, if spoken seriously, would have required heads to be chopped off.

The amazed thought about the implications of that was still in his mind when the comic drama ended as abruptly as it had begun. Lilgin raised his hands and clapped them. The echo of giant hands clapped thunderously from the ceiling.

Krosco stiffened. He had been leaning forward. Now, he straightened excessively. His eyes closed. He put his hands in front of him like the stereotype of the sleepwalker. He turned. And like a sleepwalker, or – better – a hypnotized person, walked to the door by which he had entered; and, continuing to make like a robot, pushed it open, and walked through and beyond. It swung shut behind him.

Everybody stood up . . . End of meal, thought Orlo; and started to rise, also. He was relieved. It looked as if he would actually get out of here with his skin intact.

The thought ended. The hand of the man to his right had reached over, and was grasping his shoulder; holding him down.

'You are about to be toasted,' the man murmured. He was middle-aged and determined looking in some way and with a familiar face – he must have been on television as a government representative. How he had survived to his present age was not clear.

Orlo blinked. And felt the blankness envelop his brain. But he remained seated, as directed.

A magical event. All those faces looking at him. Lilgin, directly across from him, standing also. So this is why he had me sit here – Lilgin's black eyes glinted as with an inner light, pointed at him. The great man's black moustache stirred, and the slit of mouth under it crinkled into a smile.

Then the mouth opened wider, and said in the well-known oratorical style, 'I propose a toast of welcome to the new member of the Supreme Praesidium, who will have the title, Scientist Intellectual, and be spokesman with and for the division of technology and science, with his headquarters in Communications City. I give you . . . Orlo Thomas.'

Once more, the smile. Then the glass came up to the lips. As Orlo watched, petrified, everybody drank, and looked at him. Several said, 'Hear, hear.'

'Now,' murmured the man beside Orlo, 'respond.'

The process of what Orlo did internally during the seconds that the toast had been drunk, was a significant tribute to the thousands of hours that he had devoted to preparing himself for – rebellion.

In the act of standing, he regained his awareness that obviously this was part of a game, and that he intended to be a principal player even if his game lasted only a day or an hour.

Fleetingly, in the back of his mind, was the further awareness that this was not a promotion he would turn down. Because it could theoretically multiply his opportunities to overthrow the regime.

He sensed the return of composure. And he smiled. He raised his own glass. He said:

'Gentlemen, one of the greatest problems in this world is the difficulty of knowing truth or speaking it. For some reason, which is not clear to me, I have an intense need to say exactly what I believe. At the moment, I am dumbfounded at the honour which is being done me. I hope that those persons who are responsible for this honour are prepared at all times to hear exactly what I believe about any given situation. But they may rest assured that I shall only speak my belief when I am asked, and then only in reply to a specific question. Thank you.'

He lifted his glass, and touched his lips to the rim. And then he smiled, and asked, 'And now, where do I sleep tonight?'

Lilgin laughed. It was audibly a spontaneous amusement. Whereupon, a wave of laughter rippled around the table. When it had subsided, the dictator said genially, 'My young friend and colleague, I shall have General Hintnell escort you to your new apartment.'

He looked around. 'All right, gentlemen, see you all tomorrow night here at dinner.'

With that chairs moved, and people broke from the table. The big doors opened. Egress began. Orlo glanced at his watch. It was 9:22.

As he himself headed slowly for the doors, he looked around for Lilgin. But the dictator was nowhere in view.

Before he could think about that, fingers touched his elbow. 'This way, Mr. Thomas.'

Orlo turned. The youthful general stood there. 'Are you, uh –' Orlo hesitated, then '– uh, Hintnell?'

'Yes, sir.'

'You're to take me to my apartment.'

'I have the key here. And if I may say so, sir, congratulations.'

'Thank you.'

'I shall,' said General Hintnell, 'take you to the door. Those are my instructions. You will enter by yourself. From there on, you are expected to take over.'

It was an odd way of saying it. And, since they were walking along the corridor now, Orlo silently considered the wording . . . I'll be damned, he thought finally, now he's got me worried again – What could possibly be in his apartment that he needed 'to take over'?

He remained silent as they went by elevator to the third floor of the four storey palace. Out, then, onto another huge corridor, and along it to a door that had on it in gold letter and figures: C 28.

The grim-faced young super-officer stopped; and there for a moment they stood, the two of them . . . Two youths, thought Orlo, barely out of our teens – and Hintnell was a general, and he was a Praesidium Member.

The deadly significance of it did not seem to strike the young general. 'This is as far as I go,' he said. He held out two small metal prongs attached to a silver-coloured chain. Orlo recognized the prongs as the type of electronic device that could be attuned to an individual's electro-magnetic field, and would thereafter operate only for him.

'They're duplicates,' said General Hintnell. 'So keep one in one place, and another elsewhere. A second set may not be easy to come by.'

Orlo took note of the advice. He deduced that keys to these apartments came from Lilgin himself. And that the great man would be critical of a Praesidium Member who lost small items like keys.

The general was backing away. His stern face remained enigmatic. His grey eyes did not blink. His sturdy body was held firmly erect. Abruptly, he saluted, swung about, and strode rapidly off down the empty corridor.

Orlo waited until the uniformed figure disappeared around a corner. Then he did the attuning pressure thing on one of the keys. Then he unlocked the door –

And pushed it open with one foot, warily.

TEN

As the heavy door swung open, Orlo saw, first of all, that the lights were on inside. And that was immediately a plus-factor.

It could be, he thought, that Lilgin himself is in there, come in for that 'chat' . . . If so, how would the dictator judge a young man who entered an apartment in the palace (the guarded, enormously protected palace) so cautiously?

He knew why. Everything that had happened was unreal. In fact, it had no visible, logical explanation . . . I suppose I should just go in and to hell with it, because the whole thing makes no sense – besides, the truth was (a sobering realization) that if anything official was waiting inside to overwhelm him, there was nothing he could do to stop it.

It was a feeling analysis that probably would have prodded almost any other bold youth into action. But Orlo wasn't moved by it. There was another truth in him. He was a counter. He counted things that he could see, and he counted risks mentally in advance. As he stared now through the open door into the interior, he was counting the fantasticness of what he saw.

Such a room as was partially visible to him, standing there, he had never seen in his entire short life. Furniture utterly costly looking. Carpets bright and thick and rich. He counted the length of the living room that he could see as not less than seventy feet. In the distant background was a view window, gloriously large.

Me! This has been assigned to *me* by the dictator of the world – why?

It was a 'why' that would be there for the hours and days ahead, always tugging at his reason, always incredible and suspect. And for long, for desperately long, with no answer.

Because there was not a clue to the truth in his conscious awareness, and no one visible in what he could see of that great, wonderful room beyond the door, Orlo walked in.

He could have tiptoed across the threshold. He could have peered around the door jamb one way, and through the crack at the hinges the other. But his feeling, now, was: since I don't know anything about the improbable things that are happening, and since I have now counted some of the possibilities, let me be calm again, and take it all stride by stride.

That's what he did next. After so much hesitation, he strode in.

In a kind of a way, then, he did half-expect to see Lilgin. Thus, because he was looking for a small, elegant male with black hair and black moustache, it took a measurable number of seconds before he saw a brightly dressed girl with long blonde hair.

She sat sort of curled up on a richly coloured divan off to his right. And the outfit she had on sort of matched the colours of where she sat. It was the chameleon principle at work, like a yellow worm sitting on a yellow leaf. And, of course, her startlingly goodlooking face (which did not match the leaf) was the first part of her to leap out, so to speak, at him.

After that, the rest of her came into view rapidly.

She said something at that point – probably her name, Orlo realized later – but at that instant he was staring, and didn't hear it.

For some reason, her next words were clear and totally audible. She said simply, 'I was asked if I would like to be the girl friend of a new man in the palace. And, of course, I thought it would be unwise to refuse. So if you agree, I get to stay here from now on.'

He thought of her in those first moments after she had spoken as an *agent provocateur*. A spy. And then he looked at her again. This time he noted that she was probably not more than eighteen or nineteen.

With that observation, Orlo turned and closed the door behind him. Then he turned and walked over to a chair near the divan where she remained curled up. And he sat down.

It was not impossible – his first suspicion. She could still be the eyes and ears of a dictator, and later could be a witness. But her age marked her as merely another dupe. She was, like him, someone caught up in the forever dark purposes of the most remorseless man in the history of the world. Soon, she would have forbidden knowledge in her pretty head. Thus, whether she was innocent as her words implied, or guilty as he had initially believed, the end-result would be the same. She was doomed. Her living days could be numbered in weeks, or months; surely no more than a year. Her destiny was an early grave.

He had braced himself many times against such malignant visions. It was not hard to brace himself again. Also, he was curious. 'How was it done?' he asked.

'What?'

'Getting you over here?' When she looked blank, he went

on, 'You know, who gave you the assignment to come over here to this apartment?'

'Oh!' She brightened. 'I was called into the commissar's office – where I work – shortly before five, and told.'

'You didn't argue?'

The pretty face looked baffled.

Orlo continued, 'You didn't say, "I'm a girl whose body belongs to herself, and it is not available to be assigned to a stranger." '

Her bright eyes stared at him. 'Are you out of your mind?' she said. 'I've never belonged to myself since I came out of the mists of babyhood and found myself a member of my first group. We were an intercontinental organization – we were told – all of us devoted, eagerly serving the people. After I had been indifferent a few times, and acted as if my own personal whims were more important than the group purposes – and each time I was penalized – I got the message. And so within months, before I was five years old, I developed a joyous smile and the ability to vibrate with group energy. I never actually opposed anything after that. Yet I was thinking my own thoughts all the time, observing, considering, but accepting since there was no escape from my group obligations.'

In case anyone was listening, Orlo spoke the stereotype: 'Most people, when they grow up, cooperate with their employer for a salary, with a woman or a man in the marriage situation, and with friends in order to have companionship. They behave in stores and in other public places. They pay their bills. And so on. Why shouldn't all this be observed by a social engineer like Lilgin, and made a part of larger group activity by law? By that method, individuals who would normally be dissidents are forced to cooperate, also. And that is the main purpose of the system: to catch that percentage of troublemakers.'

The girl looked at him. Her eyes were slightly widened, and so he had his first impression of their colour: hazel. But she said nothing.

'However –' Orlo continued, '– what you have been assigned seems to go considerably beyond lawful group activity. I'm sure you could complain to your street government.'

'I had to report to them when I moved my things,' she

said. 'The secretary there authorized a taxi at the street's expense to take me over here. She made no comment. She just did it fast.'

Orlo leaned back in his chair, closed his eyes, and said, 'How did you get into the palace grounds? Did you have a written authorization?'

'How else?'

'The guard at the palace gate looked at it, and waved your taxi in?'

'No. The taxi had to stop right there and turn around. My bags were put into a conveyance, taken to an inspection station, and what was in them was examined piece by piece – by hand and – and by those, uh – you know –' She made a vague gesture.

'Electronic?'

'Yes.'

Orlo opened his eyes. 'I can see,' he grinned, 'that a girl who can't even remember the word, electronic, will be an ideal companion for a person like myself.' He explained, 'I'm trained as a sort of scientific supervisor. I'm a jack of all sciences, master of none.'

'I'm totally ignorant of science,' she admitted. 'I was barred at school from all that. So I got the message early, and blotted it out whenever I came into accidental contact.'

It did not at that moment occur to Orlo to ask what her training was. He realized he was shocked by the arbitrariness of those persons who had pointed a direction for her education, and had never let her deviate from it. He shrugged. No use arguing with such details of life . . . Back to here and now, thought Orlo. 'Next question,' he said cheerfully. 'How did you get in here?'

'A domestic volunteer let me in.'

'A chambermaid?'

'They're called volunteers, poor things. But yes.'

Well, thought Orlo cynically, the key doesn't seem as rare an item as Hintnell suggested it was . . . He wondered if (bizarre possibility) the maid would let the girl into the apartment in an emergency, but not him. Or if that way of entrance for her was good for only one admission . . . I suppose I could give her my duplicate key –

But he made no immediate move to do so.

Aloud, he said, 'What do you think would happen if I told

you that I don't believe in women being furnished to men as prostitutes? And asked you to leave?'

'I suppose I'd have to go. But please don't send me away tonight. I have no authorization to be anywhere else.'

'Oh – that,' said Orlo, resignedly.

'Besides,' she spoke hastily, 'I'm not here as a prostitute. I still have to work daytimes to earn my living. I get no extra pay for this. So I've labelled myself mistress. I'm hoping you'll do the same.'

It was an appeal. Her voice had a tiny begging note in it that jarred him. 'Okay, okay,' he said wearily, 'you sleep in the bedroom. I'll stretch out here on the couch while I think all this over.'

No more than ten seconds after those accepting words were spoken, the girl moved her body for the first time. She began to uncurl. Orlo watched sympathetically as she unwound from her defensive position, and lowered a pair of shapely legs to the floor. 'I'll sleep on the couch,' she said, firmly.

He shook his head. 'Don't be ridiculous.'

'It's one of those apartments,' she said, 'where you get to the bathroom through the bedroom.'

Orlo was abruptly amused by the implied logic. 'What does that mean?'

'We might as well recognize that intimacy is inevitable.'

He grinned. 'I guess I can go through the bedroom without pausing to lie down.'

'You're dreaming,' she said. 'You can only do me harm by resisting this situation.'

He had no real answer to that. His feeling was that she was doomed now whether she stayed or went. But it was possible that if she left in the morning she just might survive. He braced himself in his fashion against the instant gloom that thought brought, and said, 'I gather you've looked the place over.'

'Your bags were here,' she said. 'I unpacked them, and put your things in the bureau drawers in the bedroom. What will you be? Some sort of young people's official in the palace?'

'Something like that,' said Orlo.

She said, 'There are extra blankets in one of the clothes closets, the – you know – kind.'

'Electronic?'

She nodded rapidly, and stood up. Erect, she looked about 165 centimetres to his 180. She must have had a similar awareness. 'We're a good fit,' she said, 'for a man and a woman.'

'You seem to speak with the voice of experience. I personally have never had a woman.'

'I've never been authorized before either,' she said.

'You're a virgin?'

'What else? If you're even seen talking to a boy your own age, you get a lecture from the street government about the importance of preventing over-population.'

Orlo was smiling grimly. 'Since contraceptives are provided only for married couples, what would our method be if we accepted this situation?'

'I was sent to a doctor before I came here. He gave me some pills.'

When Orlo said, 'I thought things like that weren't good for the health!' the girl shrugged. And when he said, 'You've taken one?' she nodded.

Then she said, 'Would you like to see the bedroom?'

'Not really. Not tonight, except for having to go through it to the bathroom, and for getting ready for my couch. I'm tired. No sleep last night, and a long day.'

'Oh, you poor thing. Of course.' She sounded contrite. 'I should have realized.'

'Get my pyjamas, a pillow, and a blanket,' Orlo said. 'I see three doors besides the one to the hall. Which one leads to the bedroom?'

She pointed. 'That's a kitchen.' She pointed again. 'That's a sort of an office-library. And –' Vision, then, of the girl in colourful coat and slacks hurrying toward the third door. She opened it, and held it for him as he went in. In the act of entering, Orlo caught his first glimpse of the dazzling interior. He faltered, but only for a moment. Then he was walking, eyes pointing straight ahead, toward the only other door that he could see.

It turned out to be a bathroom with a small swimming pool for a bathtub, gold coloured taps, a shower for two, *two* toilets, four washbowls, and drawers by the dozen, plus half a dozen mirrors of various sizes. As Orlo stood helplessly surveying the shining, gleaming, glistening everythingness of it all, the girl brought his pyjamas, handed them to him, and said, 'You'll find the blanket on the divan where I was sitting. Is that all right?'

The tiredness was back. He said, 'Fine.' He thought with a wan smile: In the morning I'll make up my mind about why it's all right for her to stay . . .

Morning. His watch said ten to eight . . . Boy, it's time I was up.

He rolled out from under the blanket, and sat up on the divan. He picked up his clothes from the nearby chair, and went through the bedroom to the bathroom. As he did so, he was aware that the blonde person in the king-sized bed was awake. The memory of her too-wide eyes (with fear in them) went with him. While he dressed he tried to recall what she had said her name was. And that brought the realization that she had probably told him in her very first words, the ones he had missed. Yet, a magical thing was happening. Something was coming out of that amnesic moment – Shala, Shala – Shanta, Shanta – Wonta, Wonta – could it be that her identity was in one of those words?

He gave up presently. He could always ask her. And, in fact, since he would have to talk to her and tell her what his decision was about her, that was the best idea.

He bathed, shaved, combed his abundant hair, zipped himself into cunningly designed clothes – and came back into the bedroom feeling clean-cut and nattily dressed, and with the faint smile of somebody who was not fooled by anything or anybody, and intended to stay that way.

He stopped at the bed and looked down at the good looking blonde girl who lay in it, staring up at him. 'Hi, kid,' he said.

'Hi.' She spoke shyly.

'What's your name?'

Her eyes brightened with understanding. 'Oh, so that's your problem,' she said.

'You got me wrong, kid,' said Orlo. 'I don't have problems.'

She said, 'My name is Sheeda.' She added, Are you going to be my brother?'

She was smarter than he had imagined. It was an insightful question; and he respected the sharp observation behind it.

'Why do you ask?' said Orlo, curious.

'Once you get to be a brother, it's hard to be anything else.'

'Don't you think that's the best solution for us here? Took me most of the night to decide that.'

She sat up abruptly. 'Then I get to stay?'

'You understand fast,' Orlo smiled.

'That's all I've got –' She tapped her forehead '– a quick mind.' Her perfect, oval face was brighter. She said, 'Maybe between the two of us, with your slow mind and my quick one, we can solve the mystery of human nature.'

There are some people, thought Orlo, who are naturally irritating, and have a propensity to show their ability at it every eighteen seconds. And maybe I've got one of that kind here . . . Aloud, he said, 'What makes you think I have a slow mind?'

'You said it took all night for you to make up your mind. Why did it take so long?'

'A quick mind like yours,' he retorted, 'should have figured that out long ago.'

'I'm sorry you're angry with me, brother,' she said. 'In the future I'll try to be properly sisterly.'

Orlo said, 'Good.' And turned away.

He went out of the apartment without a backward glance. But he was impressed.

ELEVEN

Orlo emerged onto that fabulous corridor, and closed the apartment door behind him. He did not exactly pause then. But, as he walked slowly towards the elevator foyer, there was, in effect, a prolonged pause inside him.

During that pause, he was not unaware of his surroundings. He couldn't help but notice that the gleaming marble wall opposite, was not as distant as downstairs – thirty feet compared to forty on the first floor. And he was almost literally shocked into an awed consciousness of the distances of the corridor itself: a thousand feet, at least, in one direction, and about four hundred to the elevators, in the other.

The fact was, in spite of his inner effort not to be disturbed, the vastness of the place and the enormousness of what had happened, overwhelmed him. Because – what next?

As he walked, he was grimly amused at the way he had wasted the previous twelve hours – Gave all my spare moments last night, he thought, to deciding it was better for Sheeda to stay (for the simple, stark reason that there was probably no way to save her now unless he saved himself) – so that he hadn't had time to consider his own immediate future.

There in the great palace walked this youth, Orlo Thomas, trying to make meaning of what had happened. He was almost totally out of his element. Until two days before he had been thousands of miles away, nerving himself to fight a protest-level battle against the system. He had been a tiny figure struggling in a vast ocean of people to point out to other tiny figures near him a dictator's scheme.

He believed that he had figured out at age fifteen the dirty method by which the all-powerful Lilgin utilized unknowing teeners who were stricken with chiefism to replace the older men who had caught onto the swindle and had to be disposed of. A few years later *that* crop of vain youths would have to be deposed for the reason that they, also, had suddenly understood the awful reality.

Orlo's personal predicament was far worse than he knew, or could yet know. He was completely unaware that the night before at the dinner he had met, not Lilgin himself, but his principal alter ego. The dictator had no intention of exposing himself to a meeting with Orlo Thomas. The Great Big Genius believed that the unsuspecting youth could not possibly guess the truth during the three days that remained until his 21st birthday.

Twenty-one years after birth was the most likely of a number of dates that a computer had selected – on the basis of other closely watched actions of Orlo from the moment he was born – as being the time of decision. Everything had been done accordingly: the offer of a promotion in his job, the expected rejection, the reaction to that rejection. Step by step, day by day, moment by moment, the victim's remaining seventy-two, or -three, or -four hours of life would be monitored right down to the minutest act or word. He was bugged, the girl was bugged, everyone who might speak to him was bugged, his apartment was bugged. There was no escape. Death would strike the instant the secret of the Pervasive system was seized.

Unfortunately, Higenroth nearly 22 years before had decided that the alter ego idea was too complex to program into a newly formed embryo. So that mystery and a few other confusions a bright young man would have to solve himself – so Higenroth had reasoned long ago because he actually had no choice.

There was a rather fine looking man in the elevator when it stopped for Orlo. He looked to be in his forties, and had been an attendee at the dinner the night before. He smiled and nodded at Orlo, and said, 'Well, well, you start high.'

'How do you mean?' Puzzled. Momentarily distracted.

'I've just been upstairs to see The Boss. Now, on returning down to my level, I discover you've been assigned a third floor apartment.' He explained, 'The higher your floor the better your view the greater your status. I'm a second storey man myself, after fifteen years.'

Orlo smiled back. 'I didn't get a chance to look at the view. My attention was elsewhere. Maybe, we should switch.'

'Is she pretty?' asked the older man in a significant tone of voice.

'Well . . .' began Orlo diffidently.

The other seemed not to notice, or, if he did, pretended not to understand, the hesitation. He said cheerfully, 'I really don't need to ask. The Boss probably knows where the most beautiful females on the planet are located, and he assumes that the majority of them would like to be near the centre of power, and that they will adjust to almost any man of reasonably acceptable appearance if status goes with it. I believe he's right on that. Certainly, the girls I've been assigned have adjusted rapidly.'

The elevator had stopped by the time that was said, and the door was sliding silently open. 'May I ask, sir,' said Orlo quickly, 'what your name is? I apologize for not knowing. Your face is familiar, but –'

'No problem,' was the smiling reply. 'Can't know everyone. Praesidium Member Aldit Apton.'

Having given his name, he bowed, and walked out, and off.

Orlo emerged from the elevator interior more slowly. And he did not know, or think, that the meeting had not been an accident. That its sole purpose was to feed his ego: oh, boy, a third floor apartment, to start. Such a thought in his head would add its twisting power, and help float him up somewhere away from his enormous quota of good sense.

Thus, the seed was planted, and he didn't notice.

As he walked, now, on the broader main floor, his pace was a little more confident, spurred by the 'chance' meeting. Suddenly, everything felt more real inside him. A member of the Praesidium had recognized him as a colleague. For some reason the dictator favoured him. Upstairs was a girl with a top-level biting – but humour, intellect and a body made of roses and orchids.

Why don't I, he thought ebulliently, go to Communications City? And first of all discover if I can get in, and later discover if I can get out. And in the meanwhile take a look around and see if I really do have a headquarters over there. The words about that had been spoken by Lilgin in a fairly precise fashion. Maybe it was all there, and all real, too.

Just like that he had a goal. A place to go. To be. Inside him the . . . pause . . . ended. Action, movement, a sense of life resuming – completely false.

But it felt good.

A member of the Supreme Praesidium of an entire planet does not move anonymously through a Central Government Building. Unknown to Orlo, at the dinner when he was toasted, and during his answer, his picture had been taken by hidden cameras. The entire sequence was already on television, and of course it had been flashed at once to all personnel in the palace.

On the main floor there were people everywhere. Of those, some were civilians and some soldiers. They were not just ordinary soldiers, these last – except for the guards in front of certain doors. Those who walked the hallways were arrayed, of course, in the ugly uniforms affected by all military 'servants of the people.' Epaulettes told the rank of an individual. In the course of ten minutes Orlo was smartly saluted by three generals, and a variety of lesser (but potent) armed forces officialdom. And each of the more than a dozen civilian men and women Orlo passed went through a process of suddenly becoming aware of him, hesitating, and then bowing, and walking on.

By the time he arrived at where the palace joined by way of a corridor that scientific centre known as Communications City, Orlo was not surprised when the guards all jumped smartly to attention. Also the officer in charge said, 'Yes, sir!' to his question, 'And very well, sir!' to his request, and 'I'll have a platoon guide you to your office, sir.'

Minutes later, while striding along with the little troop that was doing the guiding, Orlo met two of his day-before luncheon companions. He had left the table at the time, knowing only the names of Ishkrin, Peter Rosten, and Anden Duryea. The two he met he could mentally place in their seats in relation to where he had sat, but he didn't know name or professional training of either. (The men were the red-haired McIntosh and the black biologist, Yuyu. And they were strolling together along the wide hallway.)

For a fateful set of seconds, Orlo did not realize what his situation must look like as seen by a bystander. Did not realize that to the men it must seem as if he were being forcibly escorted.

What he did observe was that both men stopped. Their eyes widened. Then they looked at each other. In that look, as events quickly established, was evidently an agreement that needed no prolonged intercommunication.

The fundamental reality was that he had made a favourable impression on just about everybody at the luncheon. And these doomed men, living their useless lives – or so it seemed to each individual – had gazed the day before at his bright young face and had realized what a sharp mind he had. And so, just by being that young and that smart, he had got to them. What he got to was the secret place where each man kept enshrined what remained of his fight to give a personal meaning to life.

The consequences of their chance meeting with Orlo would, of course, have been nothing if they had been ordinary men. But they weren't. They were super-scientists.

Capable, highly trained technologists who were in Communications City because they were above average. They could think and they could do.

At the moment they were not thinking too well. They

were feeling. It was a feeling of intense motivation, with years of suppressed rage and resentment to drive it. What that motivation did: each man produced a defence that he had privately prepared for a moment of crisis, or confrontation, that he had bitterly envisaged for himself. As vaguely foreseen by him, he intended to go down fighting. Now –

Yuyu said, 'This is too much, Mac. I won't stand for it.'

'That S.O.B. –' nodded McIntosh.

Those two enigmatic sentences were the sum total of their talk to each other. At that point, each man made a move with his hands, reaching – that was Orlo's after-memory – into some interior part of his clothing.

At the instant that the hands came out, Orlo felt an awful blast of heat terribly close by. As he turned, recoiling, the officer in front of him uttered a hideous scream. The scream was drowned out by a roar and billow of flame. Orlo retreated because it was absolutely unbearable at five feet, perspiringly hot at ten and when, at fifteen, he found himself with the two scientists, he stopped and took the effect of the heat; and discovered it was takeable.

For the first time, he saw that the four privates had also fallen, and were writhing in what looked like agony. But whatever they were suffering from was not the same as that which had caused the burning hell on the marble floor that had, moments before, been a lieutenant of the guard.

In a minute, the fire, having but a pile of ashes to feed on, died. Where the officer had been there was left a smouldering puddle of smoke. Only moments after that, the soldiers ceased their jerking movements, and lay still.

'Kid,' said Yuyu, 'we're sorry to have subjected you to that. But seeing you a prisoner was too much.'

Thus, belatedly, Orlo heard their truth. It seemed at once not the moment to tell his.

McIntosh said, 'They'll have been connected with their desk. So when the signal stopped, as it did a minute ago, somebody started this way. So now what?' He sounded resigned.

The black said, 'How do you want yours? Molecular or fire?'

'They're both pretty brutal,' was the reply. 'How are you going to die?'

Orlo gulped – and recovered. 'Look,' he said hastily,

'why don't you both go to your quarters? This is no time for dramatic decisions. Decide later what to do.'

'Later,' said McIntosh, '*they'll* decide.' He broke off. 'So, now you look. We can give you permanent freedom right now, too.'

They were clearly in a dark, purposeful mood; and Orlo said urgently, 'I'm going to be at the luncheon today. Be there, and we'll talk. Quick, depart!'

They were hesitant. But their faces showed that hope had suddenly come. In abrupt anxiety, Orlo grabbed both men by the arm, and literally pushed them into motion. Briefly, they held back.

'Now, before they come,' Orlo hissed.

That did it. Swiftly, the two men walked off.

Silence.

Orlo stood there in the corridor with five dead men. And he tried to think of what he would do when the rescue squad arrived. He had, as it turned out, about ninety seconds; at which time the guard captain and a half dozen men came in sight at a dead run.

Watching them come up, the youth had to admit that their appearance so promptly was a tribute to the alertness of the protective system. But he was ready for them.

To the captain – to the men – Orlo commanded, 'Provide me with another escort. And clean up this mess. Nothing must be said of this until an investigation has been conducted.'

It was, as he had suddenly divined, the right solution for the moment. Thus, almost unbelievably, he was only seconds later on his way again. This time he was guided by the captain and three of the six men.

But the problem of what to do in the long run, remained.

TWELVE

As he walked he realized there were actually two problems. One was the continuing feeling of shock at what had happened.

Later for that, he kept telling himself . . . Because the

second problem – what to do about the murders – had an urgent immediacy about it. *Something* would have to be done. What?

For several moments he toyed with a dangerous possibility: can a Praesidium member keep something like this quiet? What it boiled down to, was: could a command such as he had already given restrain the guard captain from reporting the disaster to his superiors?

Reluctantly, he saw that it was unlikely. The men would have to be accounted for. There would be a check-out point where they had checked in . . . All right, all right, Orlo thought wearily, I'll ask somebody. I'll call – who?

As it turned out, that decision also had to be deferred. For at that moment his escort and he rounded a corner. And there, directly ahead was an open door. It led into what seemed to be a large, brightly lighted main room of an office with a large staff.

Close up, the large interior turned out to be, not one big room, but a series of offices separated by walls that were almost as limpidly transparent as empty air. Three, four, or five persons were segmented into each separation. And an inter-office corridor ran along beside that splendid array of desks, file cabinets, and business machines beside which and in front of which and at which sat the people.

Orlo looked, and then he glanced back at the officer who had brought him here. 'This it?' he asked.

'This is your headquarters, sir. There's a Mr. Bylol inside somewhere who is the office manager. Let me locate him for you.'

'I'll find him,' said Orlo. 'You may return to your station.'

He watched the troop march smartly off. As, a moment later, he started along the sub-hallway of the interior, a door at the extreme far end opened suddenly. A lean man emerged from it and came hurrying forward. He arrived breathless, one of those high-colour, smooth face, partially bald types. He vaguely resembled a couple of bookkeepers that Orlo had seen in the course of his brief post-college career.

'Mr. Thomas,' he gasped, 'I was just now advised that you were coming. My apologies for not meeting you at the door. I'm Mr. Bylol, your administrative assistant. Permit me to show you around.'

Orlo was, of course, willing to grant that permission.

. . . Question (somebody must have asked it): how much of an office do you give a man who has two or three days left to live? – Answer: if he's twenty years old, and you want to delude him, you make it larger than his expectation, and include space for it to grow into, as if he has a future.

Orlo walked from one department to another, trying to grasp the idea of each: Physics, mathematics, electronics, photography, biology, astronomy, rocketry, transporter, engineering, energy – at that point he came to the empty offices.

Mr. Bylol explained, 'We'll have more staff in here in a couple of days. I understand there's a new project.'

'Yes,' nodded Orlo, trying to remember what it was. It had been named at the scientist's luncheon the day before. But he couldn't remember, except –

'Higenroth,' he said.

'The Pervasive System,' smiled the lean man, rubbing his long, thin palms together, expressively.

Orlo had to suppress an impulse to act knowledgeable. He was astonished at himself, and thought: let's not pretend to be aware of something we know nothing about . . . Aloud, firmly, he said, 'Later, I want to be briefed on that.'

Mr. Bylol smiled again. 'We're ahead of you. Summaries have been prepared. But, of course –' the smile faded '– your secretarial staff can only go so far. In the final issue –' apologetically '– the scientists themselves will have to be your source of data.'

Orlo nodded his acceptance of the 'of course'. In the nod was in addition his acceptance that all these secretarial people were indeed at his disposition. And also there was in his nod an attempt to agree that the entire office and the equipment in it were equally in his total control.

He was inside one of the offices as he had that final thought. Instantly, a curiosity that had been hovering at the edge of his mind throughout the tour came to full awareness. He said, 'What's in those filing cabinets?'

At once, he decided that a question was not a sufficient expression of the power of his control. So he walked over and pulled open a drawer. It was marked 'Confidential – to be opened only by authorized personnel'. The drawer moved weightily to his pull. Far more important, no one budged.

The two young women and the slightly older man who had stood up as he came in, remained where they were, and at attention. And Mr. Bylol stood rubbing his hands and smiling his smile.

Satisfied, Orlo looked down at the solid pack of plastic files inside. Deliberately and at random, he drew one out, took it over to a desk, sat down, and scanned through it.

Reports.

Minute by minute accounts of the last day of Professor Dun Higenroth, as described by various persons, and by lengthy interviews with Eidy.

Since it was not the kind of detail that a top executive would be expected to give attention to, he merely identified what it was; did not, himself, read any of the papers. He closed the file, retaining an impression of thoroughness and exhaustive detail of what it contained . . . All right, he thought, so everything that's known is here in this series of offices and in the various cabinets. So that's my first project. On how expeditiously I handle it may well depend my chances of staying on here long enough, until I can size up this entire situation.

It was the first dim shaping inside him of a sort of long term plan. A mistake, of course. Truth was he would have to do much, and do it fast. But it was the kind of decision which people under tension can be detoured into. Avoidance. Waiting instead of acting.

The immediate consequence: a pressure that had been deep inside him ever since at age fifteen he had his Great Thought about Lilgin and his Teenage Dupes . . . let up a little.

The bookkeeper type now led him along the connecting sub-corridor to a door that opened into a room, the walls of which were not transparent: 'Your private office, sir.' Actually, the beginning of it was an anteroom office with three young women in it, along with desks and cabinets. They, of course, got to their feet quickly, and smiled acknowledgement as their names were spoken, and bowed a little to indicate their state of subordination.

Next destination was another door. This led to an inner secretarial office where a single young woman sat behind a somewhat larger desk, surrounded by somewhat more complex equipment: an intercom viewplate, a small switchboard, a private system of copying important documents. This young woman also leaped up, as the two men entered. She was black-haired with a full face and a good figure, and familiar looking. Bylol was starting to introduce her, when Orlo recognized Lidla.

That's funny, he thought. How did she get in here?

He stepped over in front of the desk, behind which she stood. 'I want to thank you,' he said, 'for your kindness to me last night.'

Lidla glowed. But Orlo, the way he was standing, could also see the girls in the outer office; and they were wide-eyed, visibly envious. To them what was happening must seem fantastic. A secretary being spoken to on a personal basis by a member of the Praesidium. The history of the new member's connection with the dictatorship was unimportant, at this level of life. They undoubtedly presumed that merit was involved. Already, the background of the promotion he had received was vague, if indeed its details were even guessed at.

The fact is, Orlo thought ruefully, the background is not even known to me . . .

There was no time for him to pursue his initial puzzlement about Lidla so coincidentally having been selected to be his private secretary. Bylol had opened a door beyond her desk, and was beckoning. 'Sir,' he said, 'your office.'

Orlo saw, first, a gleaming hardwood floor, and he had a sense of a large room. Inside, was lavishness equal to that of the apartment he had been assigned in the palace. Both side walls of the enormous inner room were book-lined. The rear wall consisted of a full-length view window, with French doors leading out into a section of garden. And there were two other opaque doors, opening – by God! – into a kitchen and a bedroom.

It was suddenly like another apartment. The bedroom had the same wall-to-wall carpeting, and the additional throw rugs. And the wall hangings, subdued lights, and a king-sized bed made the place a virtual duplicate of what he already had in the palace. It was a second place to sleep, and eat, and live – if he wished.

What was so ironic: at eighteen, after leaving the home of his parents (the Thomas's) as required by law for both youths and girls reaching that age, he had been assigned a one-room cubbyhole. The condition was labelled, *First Step to Independence*. The tiny place was in a long, drab building containing similar cubbyholes, on a street of similar buildings. The area had shopping centres and other facilities devoted exclusively to single men. It was a restricted section. At night one needed authorization to leave it.

Miles away across town there was a similar apartment complex for single women. The bridge between the two groups was a mating computer. To this machine one wrote an application stating one's personal qualifications and requirements, and asking permission to marry.

From *that* within the space of two days, to *this*.

After so much fantasia, it wasn't easy to compose himself. But Orlo tried. He walked to the great desk in front of the enormous view window. And he sat down in the gorgeous imitation-leather chairs, leaned back, testing the feel of it. He tried the drawers. Each had its supplies – which he did not check to see what they might be. Just – he noted – there it all was.

During these moments his mind was working feverishly. And so now he made a decision. It was his intention to have lunch with the same group of scientists as on the day before. He therefore told Bylol to reserve his place for him at that table. And when that had been done he asked the man to have one of the girls bring him the basic, overall summary of the Higenroth matter.

The girl who brought it was Lidla. And so he asked her the question.

'I volunteered,' she said, 'when I saw your face on television, and realized it was you.'

'Why?'

Her face had turned a little pinker, at his first question. Now, it became red. But her voice, when she spoke, was steady. 'Everyone,' she said, 'hopes that something special will happen for them. My hope was that my meeting you alone so accidentally last night, and we speaking to each other, might lead to something special for me.'

'For example, what?'

'Being your secretary,' she said, 'is already better. But of course a woman's only hope is that a man of importance will take a personal interest in her.'

Orlo had seen it coming. But he was curious, and for

some reason not embarrassed by discussions of an intimate nature. Also, he had always been capable of pressing an argument to its ultimate reality. 'Do you have access to anti-pregnancy pills?' he asked.

'I'm sure,' she said, 'that you could have them authorized for me.'

'And you're willing to take them?'

'Instantly,' she said; and suddenly her voice was unsteady, and her brown eyes grew misty. 'For God's sake, sir,' she said, 'get them. I'm twenty-two years old, and I've been refused permission to marry, and I'll never have sex in my whole life unless you authorize it.'

Orlo sagged back in his chair, feeling abruptly limp. The emotion came at him so quickly, it penetrated his barriers. Yet presently he was able to say, 'Why were you denied the right to marry?'

'My medical record shows that there was insanity in my family on my mother's side two generations ago.'

'I see. Still –'

What he saw, grimly, was that the most insane man on the planet – Martin Lilgin – was sitting in judgement on life, deciding what should continue and what shouldn't, shaping all the races, denying, approving, refusing, authorizing, condemning, praising, and so on, *ad nauseam*, entirely on the basis of the standards that he had accumulated in his single human brain. In a way, there was nothing wrong in trying to breed insanity out of the human race, if it were in fact hereditary.

'Still,' Orlo continued, 'individuals with such backgrounds are frequently given permission to marry, provided they agree not to have children.'

The young woman said, 'I'm categorized as a mother type.'

Orlo observed that she spoke calmly and without apology. He said, 'You can't be trusted to take the pills on your own?'

'No. If I ever had the opportunity I would have a child immediately.' Again – the calm self-acceptance of her attitude.

'So I'd have to give you the pill, and stand by to see that you took it?'

'Yes.' Simply.

'Well-l-ll,' said Orlo, tolerantly, 'all this will take a while, in any event. So why don't I think about this and we'll take it up again after I've made inquiries – which I promise to do.'

'Oh, thank you.' She was suddenly in tears. 'I promise you,' she sobbed, 'I'll be a perfect mistress, accepting you totally, never taking advantage in public, calling you Mr. Thomas at all times –'

Orlo smiled. 'At least you know the requirements of such a relationship, and I appreciate that.' He reached toward the manuscript that she had laid on the desk. 'This is the Higenroth summary?'

'Yes . . . Mr. Thomas.'

'Lidla,' he said, earnestly, 'I've got to read this before lunch. There's no escape. I must know what this matter is about. So will you be a good girl and go back into your office until I call you?'

'Of course,' she said. Her hand disappeared into her bosom and emerged with a tiny handkerchief. With it she hastily dabbed her eyes. 'Don't worry,' she said, 'I'll be all right.'

Whereupon, she turned and went out, closing the door behind her.

When she had gone, Orlo had an impulse to lean back in his chair, and consider why he had not refused Lidla as completely and immediately as he had Sheeda who was more attractive both intellectually and physically . . .

He repressed the impulse to analyze because that was one of his abilities: he could put things out of mind and bring them to mind at will. Thus, he had always got things done in their proper order.

He thereupon confidently started to read the story of Higenroth. And after a page realized that his attention was not, in fact, on the subject at hand.

It was on Lidla.

Which after a little, was startling. But not, he realized ruefully, surprising.

Orlo stepped to the door, and said to Lidla, 'Ask Mr. Bylol to come into my office?' When Bylol entered in all his tall, thin acquiescence, Orlo had him close the door, and then he said, 'Please requisition a bottle of anti-pregnancy pills for me by this afternoon.'

'A bottle of how many, sir?'

'Oh –' he actually knew so little of the details of the procedure '– oh, a week's supply for one person.'

'Man or woman, sir?'

Orlo hadn't thought of the pills as being available for males. So he hesitated. He was amazed to realize that he was not that eager to ingest a drug, personally. And so, realizing, he did his bracing thing, and said, 'Come to think of it, both. But have them clearly marked which is which.'

Less than thirty minutes later, while he was lackadaisically continuing his study of the first Higenroth file, a small package was placed on his desk by Mr. Bylol's own hand. 'The female pills,' said that worthy, 'can be requisitioned on your say-so from a supply centre in the palace. These are they. The male pills have had to be sent for but will be here late tomorrow afternoon.'

That – it seemed to Orlo – told a lot about the attitudes of the men in the palace. But he merely nodded, and acknowledged, and dismissed.

When Bylol had gone, Orlo leaned back in his chair. He was aware of feeling short of breath. Once more, he realized it was wrong to choose the lesser of the two women for his first time. But there was a complex thought inside him which accepted that a good woman's virginity was more precious than a man's. Thus Sheeda must be protected. Also, at twenty-two, the older, more mature Lidla was somehow a proper subject for him to experiment with. Her act of volunteering had behind it, also, a complex condition. Not really volition at all under all the circumstances. But she believed it was; he was certain of that. So in a world where people didn't yet know why they did what they did, her willingness was good enough.

So, after reading the instructions on the bottle, Orlo touched the intercom that connected him with Lidla. When she came in, he handed her a pill. And watched as she instantly and dutifully swallowed it.

'Now,' he said, 'go into my bedroom, get undressed, get into bed; and I'll join you there in ten minutes.'

Which he did.

In less than half an hour, he was back at his desk. And this time his old method of concentration worked perfectly. He spent most of the rest of the morning on the Higenroth case. Naturally, unknown to him, the account omitted anything having to do with the switching of the Higenroth baby for the Thomas baby a score of years before. Also, he did not realize that letting him learn this much had been a sorely argued uncertainty in the dictator's mind. But in the final issue – as always – hard logic had won that silent battle.

The scheme against Orlo Thomas was extremely simple:

On his birthday (it was deduced) he would have spontaneous thoughts about the Pervasive System. These would be the explanations and suggestions that had been programmed into him long ago by his true father, Professor Higenroth. If, meanwhile, in these final days before that happened, he were intensively involved in a project on that very subject, the consequences would be a confusion between the long-ago and the now.

Thus – it was anxiously presumed – he could believe that the new thoughts were his own speculations and ideas. And he would not realize that they were a message from the past.

And, of course, regardless of what he did, or how he reacted, he would not under any circumstances have the opportunity of personal contact with the dictator.

Also, if doubt about him ever reached beyond a certain intensity, he would be killed at once.

Whereupon, Lilgin would regretfully but firmly forget about the Pervasive System insofar as obtaining its secrets depended on the son of the long-dead inventor.

The murder of the five military personnel was startling. And it immediately modified the original plan.

Two of some two hundred scientists had revealed that they possessed unsuspected weapons. It was a grave failure of security, and heads would roll presently. Meanwhile, Orlo could not again – ever again – be allowed near any of the scientists.

How could such a major modification be achieved without arousing his suspicion?

Orlo's office door burst open. Mr. Bylol trotted in, breathing hard. His eyes were wide and staring. 'Sir!' he blurted, 'my pardon. Praesidium Member Jodell is on your intercom phone.'

The man seemed overwhelmed by the eminence of the caller. He teetered there almost as if his legs were wobbling.

His mouth worked as if he were trying to speak further. Yet no more sound came forth. Speechless, he pointed at the instrument on Orlo's desk, and motioned at him as if to say, 'For God's sake, quick!'

Orlo was recalling Jodell from the dinner the night before. A heavily jowled individual about 170 centimetres in height. The man had been one of the drunken singers. Yet Orlo had twice looked up into his cold, appraising eyes that, once he was sitting, showed no sign of intoxication.

Jodell, next to Megara the most important personage in the Supreme Praesidium. Both men were of course totally subordinate to Lilgin.

Jodell – Number Three in the hierarchy of power.

Orlo felt a tremor go through him. But otherwise he was calm as he clicked on the intercom, and said to the face on the viewplate, 'Sir, I am at your disposal.'

'Are you alone?' A baritone voice.

Orlo waved at Bylol, who got the message, and sagged backward through the open doorway, closing the door limply behind him.

'I'm alone now, sir.'

'The Boss just called me,' said the big face. 'He believes it would be advisable for you to devote the next few days to the task of thoroughly familiarizing yourself with the Higenroth matter.'

'I'm reading summaries right now, sir.'

'That's only a superficial beginning.' The tone was dismissing. 'You must meet the people who were involved at the time. For example, go and see the former Mrs. Higenroth this afternoon, and talk to Dr. Glucken. And by the way do not attend either the luncheon with the scientists today or tomorrow, or the dinner with Lilgin tonight. You may attend the dinner with Lilgin tomorrow night. Let us hope that by that time you have a good grasp of this whole subject.'

It was a lot of advice and data. It implied serious shortcomings on his part. And it suggested an activity that would probably require him to go out of the palace.

As that final realization struck, Orlo experienced a distinct shock. Somehow, he had taken it for granted that he was still a prisoner on probation, and would not be allowed to leave the palace.

The next words of Number Three seemed to divine all of

these thoughts. Jodell continued, 'My young friend, your staff can requisition whatever you need: a jet to fly you anywhere on earth, military escorts, cars and guides, addresses, equipment. Everything is instantly at your disposition.' Tolerantly. 'You may even call out a battleship for a proper purpose.'

Give him apparently unlimited power. It will turn his head even more.

'I'll leave at once,' gulped Orlo. 'And thanks, sir.'

'Don't thank me,' was the reply. 'Thank the Boss. He suggested it. He seems to have taken a fancy to you. Goodbye.'

There was a click. The grim face disappeared. Orlo sat there, overwhelmed. . . . *'The Boss . . . taken a fancy to you . . .'*

I'll have to think about this, thought Orlo, shakily.

With that, he pressed a button. Which brought Mr. Bylol on the double. And thus were set in motion the forces that would enable him to carry out what The Boss had 'suggested'.

The jet would leave for the Dr. Heen Glucken home at 2 P.M. And the Gluckens had been advised, and were getting ready for the visit.

Ten minutes or so went by after that information was communicated by Bylol.

At which time a thought came that was strong enough to penetrate the over-stimulated condition Jodell's call had left him in.

Orlo remembered his *List of Admonitions*: that was the belated thought.

For five years, since the moment of his initial insight, he had written down suggestions to himself which related to the use and abuse by the dictator of teenagers. They were sub-titled: *How to Avoid Being a Teenage Dupe.*

There were only three copies of the list in the entire world. All three were written in a special code. Two were hidden. The remaining one was in his billfold. So far as Orlo knew it had never been out of his possession.

As he remembered the existence of the list, the intense excitement diminished considerably . . . Of course (he thought, chiding himself) the list applied in this situation also.

He was recalling the very first admonition even as he was in the act of carefully removing the list from the billfold. It was: 'Remember, rebels young or old do not live long. So, in a crisis you must not allow yourself to be diverted from anything that needs to be done. Do not bide your time. Be brave now.'

In all the rest of the list, which it took him many minutes to scan, there was only one other, immediately relevant statement: 'Examine the personal status of whoever gave the order that is designed to divert you. What is his power in relation to you? Can he actually penalize you severely enough to matter? What precisely did he say? Are there loopholes?'

Since age fifteen, nearly fifteen hundred nights of waking up periodically, and straining mentally, had produced bracers like that. Always in the past when the impulse had come to flinch and avoid, finding the thought that applied to the particular situation had evoked from Orlo an ever more determined stiffening of will and body.

It did its bracing now, also.

What he was being diverted from, he analyzed, was the luncheon with the scientists.

Having realized that fact, Orlo was amazed. It seemed illogical. And, when he examined his memory of the related instructions, came the additional dazzling realization: Jodell had said that. The words, as they had been spoken by Number Three, were not a direct quote from Lilgin.

It seemed to Orlo, on further reflection, that Lilgin surely wanted the Pervasive problem solved. And the scientists absolutely had to participate in such a solution.

It occurred to him, as he examined his list once more, that there were two possibilities for Jodell having taken it upon himself to forbid his attendance at the luncheon. The first possibility was that he was already involved in the game of political in-fighting: the play for power and influence that must go on all the time around an absolute dictator. The second possibility was more tolerant: Jodell, not being a scientist himself, might perhaps not realize that systems engineers like Orlo Thomas did not personally do the creative work that produced solutions.

What is Jodell's power over me? . . . Clearly, since both men were members of the Supreme Praesidium, the older could only give advice to the younger, not orders.

And, naturally, decided Orlo, nothing need be said to the scientists of an inflammatory intent. The important thing was to let them know what had happened, what was expected of them, and for everyone to be careful.

Caution! That must be the watchword.

So, the basically uncautious decision was made.

THIRTEEN

Sitting there at his gleaming desk, Orlo made an assumption:

. . . All the small actions of even a single building complex as large and important as the palace of the dictator are not under continual surveillance. Or, if they are, are not considered significant enough to report to top echelon.

Accordingly, he had Bylol call the scientists' cafeteria and move up the luncheon time of Table Seven from 1 P.M. to 12.30 P.M. The instruction was to have the table only set by that earlier hour. The food could be served at the usual one o'clock . . . Be sure to have the men who sit at Seven individually and discreetly advised . . .

At 12.22, Orlo got up from his desk, and walked to a side entrance of his office. He unlocked the door with a key that Bylol had given him. Stepped through it into a narrow hallway. And locked the door behind him. The little hallway took him several dozen feet to another locked door; which the same key opened.

What it opened to was a main corridor of Communications City.

Quietly and alone, accompanied only by a weapon – a small pistol in his right hand pocket – Orlo walked toward the scientists' cafeteria.

Orlo was not entirely surprised to see, among the early arrivals inside the commissary, both Gar Yuyu and Sandy McIntosh, the two murderers of the morning. The time was 12.27 P.M.

There were eight other men already standing around; so no special words could be spoken immediately to the two. But Orlo greeted them warmly.

Yuyu answered cheerfully. But McIntosh of the lean body, long face, and red hair was subdued and absent-minded. It was almost as if he hadn't heard Orlo's words. But he nodded, and turned away, and was thereupon the first to sit down at the table.

Orlo couldn't help but deduce from the way they and the others acknowledged his presence, sort of vaguely, that they knew nothing of what had happened. Not even Peter Rosten had apparently been advised by his friend, General Armidge. Or if he had, he was a marvel at concealment. For he walked in with Ishkrin on the dot of 12.30, shook hands with Orlo, and said, 'My friend, Ishkrin, here reported the details of your disappearance last night, and we were all worried.'

Beside Peter, Ishkrin said, 'How did it all work out?' He looked relieved. 'I'm personally glad to see you back.'

Orlo said, 'I'm going to tell my story to the whole group in a few minutes. Bear with me until then.'

The little man was amazed. 'Not even a clue for your two best wellwishers – Peter and myself. Not a single hint?'

'You'll see why in just a minute,' apologized Orlo. And repeated, 'Bear with me.'

More men were arriving. As they sat down it was apparent that the luncheon complement of Table Seven had reported in with no one more than a minute or so late. Everyone went to his place. All except Orlo sat down.

Orlo stood at his plate; and he flicked his gaze around the table trying in a single, comprehensive look to identify his companions by their locations, as he had observed them the day before.

A few names came through. So it was progress.

With that, briefly, he told them of his promotion. When he finished, there was dead silence.

They were shocked; he could see that. Here were men, brilliant, capable of rational thought on a high level, reacting to their impossible situation with the good nature of individuals who accepted that people could be unlucky – and they were unlucky. They lived in a world where a man was so insane that he believed that he had the right to total control of everybody on the planet. And they saw that this was the situation. And recognized that reason stood them in no stead. Therefore, they had adjusted, and were acting as if it was still better to be alive than dead.

But every once in a while, their defences were penetrated. And his appointment – his impossible appointment to the *Praesidium* – was such a penetration.

Silence at the table. The men looked down at their plates. There was not a smile in sight; it was almost as if breathing ceased. Orlo stopped his, watching for some kind of response.

It came from Anden Duryea. The mathematician looked up, and said, 'I've been running through my mind the probabilities in connection with this –' he hesitated '– thing. Imagine,' he said, 'a youth of twenty, whose back history shows resistance, one that attempts to defeat a basic policy which seeks to utilize the ever-young and therefore the ever-ignorant to maintain a tyrant in power. There seems to be no cause-and-effect relationship in this choice. Does the Great Man want to evaluate at close quarters someone who has come up with an awareness of his scheme? His usual method for handling dissidents, old-style or new-style, is either swift execution or swift and permanent imprisonment.'

As he reached that point, the old man glanced at Orlo. 'Where's your office?'

'Here,' replied the youth.

'I see.' Rosten nodded. 'Then you may remain a prisoner.' He was suddenly more cheerful. 'There's only one other man in the cabinet who is in any way in your situation: Megara.'

At the long table the men were beginning to stir. Heads tilted. Once more bright eyes were visible, and faint smiles twisted what had been deadpan faces.

'If only you could see,' said Orlo, 'how you gentlemen have just reacted.' He broke off, 'But before I comment on that, I'd like to ask Mr. Rosten about Megara. I thought Megara was Lilgin's most trusted associate and adviser. I had heard that on occasion when the leader is trying to solve a problem he even has Megara stay in the same room with him, so he can awaken him throughout the night to discuss the matter.'

The mathematician nodded. 'But Megara's wife, who is a very lively, compassionate woman – or was – once, just once, tried to put in a word for a friend. She was sentenced to eight years in prison. The charge was misuse of proximity to the decision maker, old-style palace politics, and influence peddling. The eight years were up three years ago, but she's still in jail; and no one dares say a word.'

The broadest smile was on the face of Sandy McIntosh. Orlo, observing it, said quickly, 'A billion in I.O.U.s for your thoughts, Mr. McIntosh.'

'What we have here,' said the engineer, 'is an extreme version of logical consistency. The old Jesuits, I believe, were the first to make that error. They would interrogate a person whom they wished to bring into their service by asking him if he believed in God. And of course in the early days of Christianity everybody had better believe in God; so our innocent would answer yes. So then would presently come the question, did he believe in an after-life? And of course he had better believe. When that was established beyond any chance of his weaselling out, the question was eventually asked, did he believe that his whole future life in heaven depended on what he did on earth? Naturally, he believed that, also. Well – to make a long story short, for those who have heard it before (I tend to be a little tiresome in the way I repeat some of my anecdotes) – in the end this kind of logic would lead our victim inexorably to giving up all his worldly goods, abandoning the ways of the flesh – including his wife and family – putting on a hair shirt under a variety of fine clothes, and devoting the rest of his life to the service of the deity.'

'What's the error in that?' asked a plumpish man at the far end of the table from Orlo.

'Never mind,' said Sandy. 'If it doesn't come to you instantly, you'll never get it. However, I will give you a clue. By that kind of logic, it's all right for Lilgin to do what he's doing.'

Of the several other comments, Chair Two, West, said, 'This is certainly an unusual event. And there will be repercussions on everyone connected to it. I strongly urge Mr. Thomas to make his will. My observation is that the younger they are the sooner they go. And he's the youngest ever.'

All too soon it was a few minutes of one, and time to stand in line for food if one didn't wish to be late. Orlo insisted on those at his table going ahead of him.

Back in his chair, with his plate scantily laden, he ate for a while; and then he said in a conversational tone, 'I wonder if I could have some thoughts about the rocket Higenroth sent up.' He was glancing around as he spoke the words. And was astonished to observe broad smiles crinkle just about everybody's face. But no one said anything.

Orlo directed his attention to the man in Chair Six, East. 'Mr. Ho,' he asked, 'what does the astronomy department have to say? If that rocket is in orbit up there, why can't we find it?'

Jimmy Ho looked amused. 'That's a lot of space up there, boy. Picture this rocket somewhere above 8,000 miles and below 18,500. The radius from earth centre would be roughly between 12 and 22 thousand miles. You can see the whole sphere could be as much as 500 million cubic miles, with the biggest segment out there above 12,000 miles. Care to go and look? Remember, Tombaugh figured there were some small moons up there. Not so small either. Five to ten miles in diameter. Nobody's ever found 'em.'

Orlo had listened patiently to the dismissing explanation. But he was actually mildly irritated. These men were giving him easy negation. 'Mr. Ho,' he said, 'I have the feeling you don't want to solve this problem. Why?'

'Now, you scare me, kid. That's power talk.'

'I beg your pardon. I don't get the logic.'

'You're throwing your weight around – I detect, after all your protests, a touch of Lilgin orientation. You are anxious to present him with a solution.'

'Just a minute,' said Orlo. He leaned back in his chair, startled, and frowning. Finally, he nodded. 'It's true. But I'm genuinely curious, also. The whole affair seems very exotic as well as being a technical mystery of the first order.'

He glanced at Ishkrin. 'Sir,' he said, 'in view of the direction this whole matter is going, what is your opinion? Should Communications City get off its good humoured behind and make haste? Or do you read this matter differently from me?'

Ishkrin stroked his moustache. He was calm; seemed to be adjudicating the question. Finally, a quizzical smile and an ironic tone as he said, 'Everyone agrees that Higenroth was a genius. But if that equipment up there ever starts to send out images, direction finders will locate it in – let's see –' He knit his brows, seemed to be thinking; then '– in approximately three seconds.' He spread his hands. 'So it ceased to be a problem when Higenroth died.' A shrug. 'What's all the fuss?'

'Has this ever been explained to his excellency?' Orlo asked.

'Several times.' The speaker was the older man in Seat Three, West.

'It should be remembered,' chimed in Yuyu, 'that the Lilgin purpose is to gain control of any perfect system of spying. Just imagine the way things are right now, and then multiply the effectiveness by about ten million Pervasive machines in all parts of the planet. Forget it, son. We aren't going to raise a finger. He's going to have to get the suckups to work on that.'

Once more Orlo swung his gaze around the table. And, with one exception, the agreement that stared back at him from all sides was a brand new idea. Until this moment, he had believed these men to be sad examples of frustrated genius. His thought had been that they should be turned loose with the tools of their trades: scopes, lasers, amplifiers, colour coders, orthicon variants, etc., galore.

But that wasn't the way it was at all.

He stood up. 'I'd like you gentlemen,' he said in a formal tone, 'to recall my back history in all this, and then consider if possibly it wouldn't be a good idea to locate that rocket in the sky. But not necessarily hand it over to Lilgin until you get your Science Magna Carta from him.'

No one said anything at all to that. He was aware of the faintly smiling faces pointing toward him, enigmatic, polite.

In scanning the expressions, Orlo found himself pausing on the one face that, a minute earlier, had not been in agreement with the others. 'Sir,' said Orlo, 'what is your name?' He gestured at the somewhat plump individual at Number Twelve West, the same person who the day before had announced plans to go to the library to 'brush up on the Pervasive theory.'

'I'm Joe Ambers,' was the reply. 'Chemical fuels.' He went on, calmly, 'The whole idea of resisting, or scheming against, the wishes of the dictator is wrong. Let Nature and the progressive discoveries of science take their proper course; and one of these days all this, too, shall pass. Sir –' he spoke directly to Orlo '– persuade these foolish men to just keep creating. Creativity, and in fact new ideas, are the solution to all problems.'

'Now, that,' said the man who sat next to Ambers, 'is either the ultimate optimism, or the best front for an administration spy that I've ever seen.'

'I suspect,' said Ambers in the same calm voice, 'that most of these gentlemen lean toward the latter possibility. I can only repeat that –' He looked around. He said, 'Nobody seems to be listening.'

'I'm listening,' said Orlo.

'I know,' said the plump man, 'but they're against you now, also. So you talking to me may now seem like a method we have devised for delivering secret information to each other.'

Orlo was mildly astonished. 'I can see,' he said, 'that there's more paranoia here than I originally suspected. I, personally, decided early that the truth of the dictatorship was sufficient. That I didn't have to, also, imagine things.'

McIntosh made a movement at that point. He said, simply, 'The truth is, lad, we can't trust you anymore.'

'It's my intention,' said Orlo firmly, 'to try to win your trust, Mr. McIntosh, and that of Mr. Yuyu for very special reasons.'

'I can't imagine,' said the lean Scot, 'what you could do that would be convincing. After all, to Lilgin the deaths of half a dozen men or half a thousand, mean nothing. To suppress or reveal, forgive or penalize, could all be part of a plan in which the fate of the people involved would be the least factor.'

Orlo had to nod his reluctant agreement to that. 'You're right, sir.' He glanced at his watch. 'I wish I could stay to see if we couldn't find a common ground, but I have to go. I can see the problem is very severe. Goodbye, gentlemen. I hope to visit with you again before my predicted demise.'

With that, he pushed back his chair, turned, and walked off without a backward glance.

Fifteen minutes later, he was climbing aboard the kind of superjet that could lift itself straight off the ground.

FOURTEEN

He sat in the hurtling machine. A king – or some unearthly equivalent.

Didn't feel that great inside, though. Instead, a puzzlement. How should he have handled the scientists?

I was caught byze – He had mis-analysed the attitudes of those angry experts – They're actually older versions of a rebel like myself; only they won't play no matter what the inducement . . .

As a consequence, he had made incredibly incautious statements.

Okay, okay – wearily – back to the drawing table.

Which, for him, meant re-examine the list. He took it out, reluctantly. Then sat there by the spacious window in the king's chair in the private compartment. And read it once more.

After a while, his seeking eyes found what appeared to be the most applicable admonition for what had happened:

'Don't question good luck. If it later turns out that the enemy is merely playing with you, see Admonition 34.'

Admonition 34 consisted of two questions: 'Why are they bothering with you? Why are they devoting their valuable time to you?'

Why, indeed? thought Orlo.

Surely, any second somebody would take action and stop all this nonsense.

But the minutes went by. And the superjet shot through the upper atmosphere faster than a bullet from a high-powered rifle. Orlo continued to sit there, watching the land far below through the view window that actually curved down to form part of the floor. Because of its shaping and its ten foot spread, he could see below and ahead as well as to the side. The air was crystal clear – which reminded him that this was one of Lilgin's achievements. Using total power and remorseless logic, the dictator banished the private automobile, modified the polluting factory, solved the problem of sewage disposal, protected wildlife and the wilderness, ended disease everywhere, fought down costs of production, provided more and more free services for everybody – if you wanted to go somewhere *for good cause* you just climbed on a plane, train, or bus (but don't take an unnecessary trip; the price might be your freedom.)

The millennium? It had the look, except . . .

Orlo had once discussed his bafflement with a 'trusted' college chum. Their conclusion: both the absolute logic involved and the resultant improvements were marvels of technology – but it was not for human beings.

Their analysis arrowed in on the basic reactions of a human baby. Pet it – and it gurgles happily. Drop it – fear. Hold it, restrain it – anger.

People were being held; and they were angry.

It was basic human nature.

'To hell with human nature!' said the idealists. 'They'll get over it, and conform!' But they said it angrily. And they struggled all the while to hold onto positions and controls whereby they did the holding instead of being among the held.

At the time Orlo's 'chum' thought better of the discussion and its conclusions, and reported it to the dormitory government. Result was a long and tiresome inquiry. And what was amazing afterwards was that, unlike certain other offenders of earlier days, he was *not* summarily dismissed from college.

. . . *Don't question good luck. If it turns out later that the enemy is merely playing with you* . . .

What then?

He was about to re-examine the illogic of it once more when he was interrupted by a discreet knock on his door. It was so discreet that it seemed without threat. But he was not a person who accepted appearances. Orlo called out: 'Who's there?'

'General Dway, sir.'

'Oh! Come in.'

The man who courteously opened the door, and entered, was the commander of the accompanying forces. He was a sturdy six-footer with a plain face and blue eyes, and a deep, soft voice.

He said, 'We're about to land, sir. Any special instructions?'

'None.'

'Very good, sir.'

Whereupon, the general departed.

Orlo sat there. And it seemed to him that, by good reason, the message the general should have brought with him, was an order which superseded his control, and placing him under arrest.

While he thought about that, the jet landed.

FIFTEEN

It was a nice enough house, though isolated. There it stood in the middle of a flatland, all by itself. It had a few trees in a backyard; and a lot of green grass, almost as far as the eye could see, testified to somebody's interest and care.

The great jet settled down about two hundred yards from the house on a particularly flat area of that meadow. And its coterie of half a dozen guard ships plopped down beside it.

As he walked toward the cute two-storey residence, Orlo wondered about its location. It would – he conjectured – be an easy place to watch.

With that thought, he stopped, and half-turned to look around. In turning, he saw that, behind him, his entourage was also coming to a halt. Until that instant he had been intent, not paying too much attention to who was following. Now, abruptly, there they were.

Orlo gazed in amazement. There were more than he could count. He estimated fifty men. They had formed a long, loose, double line; and that line stretched back to the ramp of the gleaming skyliner, with several persons still in the act of emerging from the open door.

It was a colourful array. Most of the individuals were in uniform; and different ranks wore different colours. Top officers in a light tan; junior officers in bright blue, and lower ranks in a fine grey. Several civilians – like himself – were dressed in what were essentially variations of subdued blue-grey.

An entourage. His. For a long minute, as he surveyed that

veritable throng of people, all assigned to him, ready to leap and do and fight at his command – for that minute his anxiety about his own position lessened.

So this is what it felt like – I presume I could get used to it –

The feel of power, of command.

The thought lasted moments only. Then: of course, he thought, being against such presumption is why I'm here . . . He was abruptly critical of himself for having wasted time reviewing the matter.

It took a minute to recall why he had stopped in the first place.

Deliberately, he sent his gaze out toward the horizon. There were trees out there. So it required time to determine where the little town was that he had glimpsed as the jet sank toward the ground.

But he located it.

It was roughly north by north-east; its outskirts a little over a mile away; several houses, now that he had located them, plainly visible against the background of greenery.

A single house to the south, a single house to the west, a single house to the east. Each about a mile distant.

Nothing in between.

Seeing it all so uniformly obvious made him feel better. The madness was real. It was not just a fantasy in his mind that people were endlessly harassed, and spied on night and day.

Like this poor couple, the Gluckens.

Orlo beckoned General Stada Dway. Dway was an older man. Presumably, he was one of the people the dictator kept around because somebody had to be old enough to know something. The general came up smartly, saluted briskly, and said, 'Yes, sir?'

Orlo waved at the horizon. 'What's the lighting situation out there at night?' he asked.

The officer's rather heavy face changed expression, transformed from alert dutiful interest and attention to a tight-lipped smile of satisfaction. 'See that line of road out there, sir, with what looks like power lines?'

Orlo acknowledged that he saw it and them. And, in fact, they seemed to be half a mile distant to north, east, and south, and west equally.

'At night, sir,' said the general, 'those roads are lighted up like day.'

Orlo accepted the information with a curt inclination of his head. But he was thinking: that guy, Lilgin, is really remorseless, just as I correctly realized long ago . . .

He was not surprised at the revelation. Knowing about such truths had been his thing since his early teens.

With that thought, he started forward again.

. . . Mother and son.

Looking at each other for the first time.

He had asked to see her first. And so here they sat now, alone, in a tastefully furnished living room with a patio visible through glass doors and windows.

The son thought: so this is the beauty of yesteryear.

Eidy was forty, almost forty-one. She had become pregnant at late nineteen, had given birth in the last half of twenty; and it was now twenty-one years plus three months later. She did not quite look her age. But she almost did.

Also, as Orlo would shortly discover, she had over the years inwardly done a peculiar process. She had got to look a little bit like her husband, Dr. Glucken. Such similarities between aging man and aging wife had been observed before by baffled students of the human equation. But the mental manoeuvres involved remained beyond the reasonings of science.

How can a woman, unrelated by blood, become physically like her husband? How can a child resemble his mother in his first five years, and then switch over to resembling his father?

People had said of Orlo that he was 'just like your father' – Mr. Thomas.

Orlo couldn't see it. But the fact was he had early acquired a liking for the elder Thomas. And he did not like Mrs. Thomas, his mother. Something about her bothered him all the time.

The woman had been impatient with him in his babyhood and childhood. And, though she had presently ceased being that way and had become affectionate, it was too late. A subconscious memory of the early years kept him alienated. He was not cruel. He either avoided her, or was courteously distant, and *never* affectionate.

Gazing, now, unsuspecting, at her son, Eidy scarcely saw

him. The sudden news that there was to be another investigation had earlier set off alarm reactions. And the feeling – intuitively sound – had come that this time they wouldn't survive.

The extreme youth of the interrogator created a temporary confusion in her. But throughout she stared at him with glazed eyes. There was something vaguely familiar about him. But the potentialities of that failed to break through her dulled resistance to what was happening. And, of course, the sensational truth was totally outside of her reality.

As he sat there looking at the woman, noticing her anxious movements, Orlo kept thinking: What am I doing here? . . . The answer echoed in his mind and was the stereotype that he was 'familiarizing' himself with the people and the known facts. A case could be made out for such a method, except (he shrugged impatiently) it was a bunch of nothing. A waste.

His impulse: To hell with it. Yet each time that feeling surged, he restrained his boredom, constrained his yawns, remained sitting, retained the serious look on his face, maintained his quiet courtesy.

And so once again the story was told of Eidy coming into the Higenroth house at the university one afternoon, and surprising her elderly husband with images on the walls. And of how the old man had asked her not to mention what she had seen.

Orlo, who that day had read a long-ago interview about that very subject, sighed inwardly as the drab account came again from the once perfect lips. It all seemed so similar. Because obviously (it was obvious to him) Eidy never had known any details. It didn't even seem to occur to her that she had witnessed a marvel of invention. As a girl and as a woman such matters simply could not hold her interest.

Yet, as others had done before him, Orlo persisted. Presently, in desperation, he was listening not only to what she said, but found himself seeking meaning from the tone of her voice; as if he would discover a clue in it to some secret memory in her brain.

In the end it was clear once more that the one-time wife actually knew less than there was to know. She had been deep asleep during the entire episode of the worldwide pervasive broadcasting of images of the dictator – the accounts Orlo had read took it for granted that it was Martin Lilgin himself who had talked to Higenroth. Neither Eidy, nor the world, nor (now) Orlo had any suspicion that there had been, or was, a duplicate of the dictator extant then (and now).

As he came all too swiftly to the point where he really had nothing more to say to this unknowing woman, Orlo hesitated; and then asked a fateful question: 'And where is your son now?'

A frightened look came into her eyes. 'B-but,' she faltered, 'what can he possibly have to do with this? He wasn't even born until a year later.' She visibly braced herself; showed visible awareness of the total unacceptability of such an answer in Lilgin-land. 'He's at college,' she said.

And then she burst into tears. 'For God's sake, sir, don't try to connect him with this.'

Orlo stood up. 'Where's your husband?' he said.

He waited while she brought the sobbing under control. He said nothing. Simply stood there. And after a little, she said in a low voice, 'Thank you.' She added, 'I'll get him.'

Orlo's interview with Dr. Glucken was equally inconclusive. In growing older Glucken had acquired a grey moustache and a slightly swollen body and face. It was easy for a perceptive person like Orlo to see what ailed this aging communications expert in relation to Higenroth's discovery. On the one hand he was bitterly jealous of it. And, on the other, he wished desperately to be knowledgeable about it.

And of course there was also noticeable in him a third condition. He also reflected in his eyes and manner the awareness that these interrogations were becoming more dangerous and threatening with each repetition.

But at least he could describe in a live human voice the Higenroth distance-zero method, upon an aspect of which – Glucken was convinced – the Pervasive System was based. So Orlo listened to that explanation; which he had first seen on the walls of Communications City, and had then seen it with charts and in summarized form in one of the Higenroth files.

A thoroughly bored Orlo presently ended the interview, walked back to his jet – with the flock behind him. He went at once to his private booth, and called Jodell.

The heavy-faced man listened grimly to his report. When Orlo had finished (without of course giving a hint of his own feelings, and in fact sounding, as the saying was, very keen), Jodell said in a voice that literally snapped it was so sharp: 'From what you say, it is time charges were filed against this couple.'

Orlo was taken aback. 'How do you mean?'

'Of all the people who conspired to conceal the Pervasive System invention, for some reason these two were allowed to tell their highly suspect story, and were not molested.'

Orlo, who had not for an instant thought of the Gluckens as being part of a conspiracy, tried to recall what in his summary had aroused such a fierce reaction in Jodell. Couldn't imagine. He saw only proof of innocence.

He ventured, 'What do you suggest?'

'Place them under house arrest. Post guards. File charges of conspiracy. I'll take it from there, and will have them transferred to a prison tomorrow.'

Orlo became aware that he had been bracing himself. The realization had come: Somewhere along here he had to make a basic stand.

He was beginning to have a horrifying picture of how swiftly an individual could become a partner in the continuing crimes of the administration . . . Boy! To hell with those S.O.B.s!

'Sir, you didn't let me finish my account.' He spoke glibly, shaking inside but utterly determined. 'I'm not through with these people. Our first purpose in dealing with them at all, as I understand it, is to get the invention. With that in mind, I want to think over what they've already said, and question them further. This may take several days. After that –' the inward bracing was at a shuddery peak '– I'll take your recommendation that they be arrested under serious advisement.'

He concluded, 'Thank you.' And broke the connection.

After a while, sitting in the jet on the way back to the palace, he felt a lot better.

SIXTEEN

The great jet made its return journey at the same colossal speed, and Orlo dismissed his entourage.

4:32 P.M.

So, now what?

He had stepped out of the jet in one of the courtyards of the palace. As Orlo walked through the nearest palace entrance, the guards there leaped to their feet, and saluted.

He was inside, buoyed, and assuming that no general order for his arrest had been issued; no charges made. He could still attempt to do what he had decided suddenly in the jet.

He walked rapidly to Communications City, returned to his office, and asked Bylol to invite Ishkrin, Peter Rosten, Yuyu, and McIntosh to come in for a scientific discussion. After fifteen minutes later, a disturbed Bylol called him on the intercom and reported that the four scientists had brought a fifth with them – a recording expert. 'They would like to have a complete recording of the interview.'

It had the look of a defensive action on the part of the men; but Orlo agreed at once. He shook hands with each of the four, and was introduced to the fifth – a man who was not from Table Seven. Chairs were drawn up, but nothing said while the interloper, whose name was Arger, placed a small array of instruments on Orlo's desk.

He was a medium-sized, jolly type. Dark-haired, brown-eyed, and with a tendency to gesture. He adjusted his tiny dials, gesture by gesture, and then pulled up a hardbacked chair and seated himself next to the desk and his equipment.

At which point he made a casual statement, and gestured at the same time. He said, 'As I thought, he's bugged, the room is bugged, the desk is bugged. It's all nullified by – I should make my confession early – me, the greatest expert in this kind of thing. I would suggest you very quickly discuss how we can give the appearance of still being bugged, and then have some buggable conversation.'

Orlo put up his hand. 'When I raise my hand like this,

Mr. Arger, that is your signal to nullify the bugging. When I hold my thumb like this, then make us all buggable again.' As he spoke, he switched to the thumb, and whispered, 'Nod, when you've done this last.'

The man did something with a tiny instrument he held in one hand, nodded – and gestured. And Orlo said, 'Well, gentlemen, I wish to welcome you here. And perhaps I should begin by outlining my reasons for inviting you. First of all, please be assured that I respect your earlier refusal to participate in the matter of re-discovering the Higenroth Pervasive System. It is my belief, however, that I have been appointed to my present eminent position for good reasons, with which – I have to admit – I am not yet fully acquainted. But it does seem to me that I should find out what the scientists are willing to become involved in. Mr. Ishkrin, may I have a comment from you?'

The great moustache and the eyes above it twinkled, as Ishkrin said in a formal tone, 'We need time to think over basic questions like that. My overall feeling is that there are many creative areas which are not sensitive. Perhaps, while I am considering what those areas are you could talk to Mr. Rosten.'

Mr. Rosten said, 'I'm just going to lean back here for a minute and think about this, and I suggest the other gentlemen do the same.' As he finished speaking, he gestured violently at Arger.

Orlo, thereupon, raised his arm.

Arger did something in his hand, nodded, and gestured expansively.

Ishkrin said grimly, 'Listen, kid, your entire situation here is illogical. Something is wrong. At this moment I don't see how we can help you, but whatever scientific knowledge can do, we can place at your disposition.'

Orlo drew a deep breath. 'I had in mind our writing messages to each other while we conducted a conversation on a more general level. Perhaps, we could combine the two. Before we switch over, my first real question is: how old is Lilgin?'

'Good God!' said McIntosh, involuntarily.

Rosten made shushing movements with his hands.

Orlo brought up his thumb.

Arger nodded, and gestured.

It was all that simple – and that complex. Each man thereafter sat with a writing pad on his lap, and occasionally scrawled furiously, or wrote deliberately while someone else was talking. Orlo did have the feeling that the verbalized part was, for the most part, exceptionally dull. It worried him a little. But what he tried for was a mention of each of a number of sciences, with an opinion from the four invited men present as to what in that science the super-experts of Communications City might be willing to research.

Since it was only cover-up, it need merely be credible to those who were listening; and any silences had to be accounted for.

As it turned out, the writing filled in most of the gaps. And he was able to limit the silences to two more.

But the writing – fantastic.

'How old is Lilgin! What's the thought?'

'The man I met at the dinner last night seemed to be in his early forties.'

'He's always looked like that.'

'Always is a long time. Be more specific.'

'The regime has existed for 106 years. The last succession took place 32 years ago. So if he was thirty then, and is sixty-two now, he could – with all those new protein injections – look forty-two.'

'Who was the previous dictator?'

'What we have here is a grandfather–father–son succession, all with the same name.'

'I presume they all looked a little bit alike, also.'

'The photographs show some family resemblance but not that strong.'

'Do you know anyone who remembers the father?'

'No, the son had everybody who ever knew the father, killed.'

'How about Jodell? Megara?'

'Well, presumably, they knew the father, and are still alive. You have to remember that these are the two biggest suck-ups in the palace.'

'What was the explanation for an hereditary dictatorship?'

'The way I heard it, in the early days of a new idealistic society, opportunists, counter-revolutionaries, bourgeoisie falsifiers, deviationists, people with a narrow understanding of realism, nationalists of all types, etc., had to be fought to a standstill. This could best be done if there was no struggle for leadership during the formative years of the first genuinely revolutionary civilization.'

Orlo grinned at that one, and wrote: 'You know the lingo even better than I do. Okay – do we have anyone who knows about those protein shots for slowing the appearance of aging?'

That got a head shake, and a quick scrawl: 'What would a diet expert be doing in Communications City?'

It was true; but – Orlo raised his hand.

'Gentlemen,' he said, 'the thought which I have had in my mind is that the whole of history refutes this concept of a grandfather, father, and son all being equally competent, equally remorseless, and exactly the same kind of bastard. My feeling is that what we have here is not just protein prolongation of life but one man who has been in power the entire 106 years. Now, how can we prove, or disprove, *that*? And where is the inventor of Martin Lilgin's immortality? Or rather, where does he get those shots and who manufactures his current supply?'

The amazed discussion of that question could have gone on a lot longer than it did. But Orlo had been keeping one eye on his watch; and abruptly he put up his hand; Arger gestured, and nodded; and Orlo said, 'Gentlemen, it's twenty-three minutes to seven. And I absolutely have to be somewhere before seven; and I imagine so do you. Therefore . . .'

He raised his thumb.

Arger nodded and gestured.

Ishkrin made some final idiotic remark about possible collaboration between the scientists of Communications City and Orlo's 'office'. That's how he worded it: office.

Orlo did not wait to find out what had happened to the staff of that office. He ushered the men out of his private exit. And departed hastily. He was thinking: it is a fact that no one person, no single human brain, can ever think of all the implications of an action. Lilgin was no exception.

The dictator had at least something that *looked* like an altruistic quality. He either gave, or pretended to give, credit to his colleagues of the Praesidium. In a special alcove on the way to the dinner room were portraits of all the persons who had ever been members of the Supreme Praesidium.

The credit part was a pretence – Orlo believed. The truth had to be over the years the dictator had had an increasing problem with memory lapses. The portraits were reminders for details that he dared not let fade. A man who forgets his enemies, and the charges against them, is in danger.

The alcove was dimly lighted. In fact, a single candle burned in front of each of the niches where the photograph was recessed so deep that a willing viewer had to stand directly in front of it to see it at all. Individuals who passed through the alcove could not help but notice the difficulty of seeing even one face, let alone all of them.

But the candle – so the story went – was a reversion to an ancient reverential symbol of admiration and friendship. The little flame, moreover, testified to the right of the individual to be respected for his personal accomplishments. Thus it was an expression of warmth and good feeling, and a tribute to the loyalty, ability, and sense of duty of him before whose portrait it flickered.

It was a quarter to seven, as Orlo walked in a deliberate way through the alcove. He appeared to be in an absent-minded state; for he stopped several times, and leaned with his back against one wall or another. Eyes half-closed (or half-open) he seemed to be thinking of something.

After a while he continued on his way. The overall direction of his motion was toward the room where the Praesidium members and the dictator and he had eaten their dinner the night before. In fact, on leaving the alcove, he proceeded briskly toward the barrier table in front of the dining room door as if he fully expected to attend. Soon, the sounds of merriment from inside were loud and unmistakable. The drunks were audibly screaming with laughter, and shrieking whatever it was they were saying to each other.

Orlo approached to within a dozen feet of the table where all the officers sat, watching him now.. Abruptly, at that point, he stopped. He did an Oh-my-God-I've-just-remembered reaction, and half-turned away. But apparently realized the amenities, and so faced the uniformed men.

He called out to the group as a whole, yet looked at the

youthful General Hintnell as he spoke: 'I've just now realized, gentlemen, that I have an urgent appointment and cannot attend this dinner tonight. If anyone asks after me, say that I'll explain later.'

With that, he turned and hurried away, shuddering at the madness of what he was doing. And half expecting to be pursued and apprehended.

When nothing happened, he grew calm again. And deliberate. Once more, he appeared to be in a series of deep, delaying thoughts as he passed through the alcove and its niches. This time he paused longest before the portrait of Crother Williams.

As in every instance, there were no dates; just the name.

The face stared down thoughtfully at Orlo. It had a slightly harassed expression. But it looked about thirty or so.

In his passage through the alcove the previous evening, Orlo had not lingered at all. But he had caught glimpses. And, during the night, had awakened once or twice and wondered about the significance of it all: the dim lights, the resultant difficulty of seeing what was in the niches; the very depth of those niches seemed meaningful.

Prior to coming to the palace, it had seemed to his sharp, suspicious mind that age thirty was just about the ultimate dividing line. As he came to that, or earlier, age, the average executive in Lilgin-land usually had charges placed against him. And he was either killed, or transported. What he was transported to depended on the charges and on his attitude. He could simply disappear into a remote hinterland into a technical activity. Or else, if the charges were especially severe – if he were, for example, charged with being a provocateur, or a bourgeoisie falsifier, or a hopelessly bureaucratic type, or showed political instability – rehabilitation could only be achieved by uncomplaining farm or other hard labour.

On this second night, Orlo took the time to observe that only about a third of the men were over thirty. He made that generalized observation while he was in the hurried act of counting the niches.

He got the unbelievable total of 284.

SEVENTEEN

It had been pitch dark for some while when there was finally a sound at the door. And, when Orlo opened it, Sheeda came in. She carried a newspaper.

'The story about you is on page one,' she said. 'Your promotion.'

Orlo accepted the paper that she handed to him. But he did not immediately glance at it. 'I notice,' he said, instead, 'it's after nine. Where have you been?'

She had been taking her coat off. Now, she dropped it into a chair and stood looking at him, a slender girl in a brown dress, her long hair like a frame for her face and neck.

'Is that a brotherly question?' she asked.

Orlo considered that. 'No,' he said finally.

'This is the night I get to be a mistress?'

He had to smile at that. 'You certainly seem to be willing,' he said.'

'I just want to stay alive,' said the girl, simply, 'as long as I can. And I have a feeling that's one of the requirements.'

'You have the wrong thought about Lilgin,' Orlo replied mechanically. 'It's his advisers we have to watch out for. He's a social engineer. They're suck-ups.'

The girl was silent; said nothing.

'Actually,' Orlo continued, 'I'm probably what would be called an idealist. I made up my mind about this woman business before coming here. It's really not good for a girl or a woman to have sex forced upon her. So it won't happen. When I look at you, I don't think of you as a sister. But I also don't believe in having a woman sent to my bed for my pleasure.'

'I still get to stay here?' she asked.

'Of course.'

'In the long run, we'll have to sleep in the same bed; so why not settle that tonight.'

'It's a magnificent double bed, large enough for two friends to bed down on. I suppose there's no reason why a youth and a girl shouldn't just room together.'

'Does that mean we sleep in the same bed tonight?'

Orlo sighed. 'You're one of those bulldog types,' he said. 'But – I suppose so.'

'So that's settled.' She was smiling suddenly. 'Why don't I make us a drink? Okay?'

'You haven't answered my question yet.'

'What question?' A blank face. Eyes blinking in bewilderment.

'Coming in this late?'

She shrugged. 'I was held up at the office. Never happened before. Boss came rushing in at five to six, and said there was some extra work that had to be got out.' She made a face. 'It didn't seem to be all that important to me, what he had me do. But you know how these sub-level executives are. They just about go out of their minds if there's any possibility of their being charged with – what is the term? – defects in their work, poor leadership qualities, or, of course, worst of all, wrecking.'

When she had finished, Orlo said in a deliberate tone, 'Never happened before?'

'Never.'

Orlo leaned back, closed his eyes. Without opening them, he said, 'Get us that drink, will you?'

It was not so much, then, that he heard her leave; that would have been a little difficult on such thick carpet. But there was a sense of emptiness where she had been that communicated to him.

That thought also faded. And he sat there, and he thought – Where was I at five to six? . . . And the answer to that was that he had been talking to Ishkrin and Rosten for over an hour by that time.

Hard to connect the two items. Presumably, he could have in his mind all through that conversation that Sheeda was normally due back at the apartment. And if it influenced him, then he would – presumably – end his meeting with the two scientists on the dot of six, and rush up to the apartment to await the girl.

But such a thought had not been in his mind. And he had not ended the conversation, and had not gone back to his apartment even when he did end it suddenly for another reason: that other reason being his plan to count the portraits in the alcove and to take a look at Crother Williams.

Besides, at no time had he known that she was being held at the office.

So she, and what she was doing, or why, was never a factor.

Yet it was. Because somebody had hastily caused her to be delayed at her office.

A total contradiction?

Actually, the logic of it was not all that difficult, or all that well thought out. When it had earlier become apparent that he was ignoring the instruction about attending the scientists' luncheon, the overall question in the minds of those who watched, and listened in, and analyzed, on behalf of Lilgin, was: What all will he do? What is he up to?

The refusal of the scientists to cooperate on the Higenroth project came as a pleasant surprise to Lilgin. Immediately, it was no longer urgent that Orlo be kept away from the prisoners in Communications City.

The girl was held up, because . . . what else does he have in mind doing this afternoon and evening? The thought was that when Orlo returned to the apartment, and she was not there, perhaps he would be motivated to reveal some additional plan or purpose. Would go and do something else.

That simple. And that unnecessary. Because on returning from the alcove, he didn't go anywhere.

Conclusion: He really doesn't understand the situation.

It was just as well, of course. The result was that the decision was reaffirmed that he would be allowed to live another day.

And that the great experiment would continue.

In the darkness there was a movement in the bed beside Orlo. Then a small womanly voice: 'Why don't you come over on top of me?'

'It wouldn't be right.'

'I think I've fallen in love with you.'

Orlo turned over on his back, and lay there under the sheets and the quilt, and was somehow aware that she had taken off all her clothes and was lying nude less than a foot away. That thought did something to him; but he braced himself against that something.

'I can't escape the feeling,' he said, 'that you believe this is something you're expected to do for me, and therefore you want to do it for fear that you'll be penalized.' He lied, 'I don't believe you will be.'

'I honestly,' came the muffled voice, 'find your attitude and restraint so wonderful that I feel overwhelmed with goodwill toward you.'

'Don't tempt me. I'm only human.'

Pause. Silence. Continuing night. Then: 'For God's sake, sir, I'm just wild with desire.'

'Sir!' he echoed. And he laughed.

It was not a long laughter, just an abrupt burst, which he hastily fought down into a cough.

'I'm sorry,' said Sheeda in a subdued voice, 'but I was told to address you that way.'

'It wasn't the word,' Orlo gulped. 'It was the context. I apologize.'

Silence. 'You say,' he said, 'you've never been made love to before?'

'No, never. So I'm curious, also. What would it be like?'

Orlo lay there in the silent darkness on the king-size bed; and he thought of kissing those sweet-looking lips, and imagined pressing his naked body down on hers. And there was no question – he wanted to, desperately.

But, also, from somewhere in the darkness of his inner being came a return of determination. Almost at once he could feel his lips tighten, and his eyes narrow. And, suddenly, there was that infinitely strong feeling of . . . No, I will not take advantage.

As he rationalized it (not for the first time): to give in to anything that was intended to corrupt, was always a mistake. True, a man should probably not deny himself sex. But truth also was, this girl was intended to start the demolishment of his purpose, whatever it might be. Therefore . . .

He said, 'Maybe if we fall in love, we should ask permission to get married.'

'You'll never be allowed to marry me,' said Sheeda. She sounded resigned.

In the morning she was cheerful again. 'I've figured it all out,' she said. 'You're probably a homo.'

Women, thought Orlo. Grrrrr! . . .

Sheeda continued, 'One has to be logical about such

things. What we actually have here is not a brother–sister thing, but sisters.'

'Grrrrr,' said Orlo again. But he said it, also, under his breath. Aloud, he commented, 'Until now I've had the peculiar belief that I might be able to talk out with you some of the problems that will surely come up in my new job. But if what you just said is a sample of your logic, I guess I'll have to forgo taking you into my confidence.'

Here immediate response to that was to go over and look out of the great window down upon the landscaped vista below. She stood there, her back toward him. She seemed to be shuddering, all the while that he put on his coat. Finally, as he walked to the door, she said without turning, 'I'm sorry. I won't be nasty again.'

'Okay,' said Orlo.

As he said it, he could feel a change taking place in him . . . For Pete's sake, he thought, what am I fighting so hard for?

He said, 'How would you like to make me a birthday present?'

There must have been a new note in his voice, for that perfect body swung around abruptly, and the blue eyes shone.

'When?' Almost a whisper.

'Tonight.'

'When is your birthday?'

'Tomorrow.'

'What would you like for your birthday?'

'You,' he said.

She was in his arms. Exactly how she got there so quickly, Orlo would never clearly remember observing. He did recall a movement out of the corner of one eye, as he turned away. But the details were simply not analyzable; at least not then.

EIGHTEEN

The dictator had awakened with a thought: that is the sharpest thing anyone has ever done, lingering in that alcove as long as Orlo did . . .

He dressed thoughtfully.

During the evening he had listened to the discussion between Orlo and the five scientists; at which time he had sent secret police to Orlo's office, and had them ransack it for scrap paper.

One crumpled sheet was the result. It had written on it in the handwriting of Peter Rosten: 'Who is Orlo Thomas? That is the real question, as I see it –'

. . . They had got that far! – So, sadly, decided Martin Lilgin.

Really amazing how perceptive people continued to be, and at the same time remained politically indifferent, showed serious opportunistic degeneration, and were cynical.

In his orderly mind, he labelled Peter Rosten's single sentence as a 'distinct enemy outburst.' He realized as he ate breakfast that he was in a state of grave doubt again. Should this experiment continue even another hour?

Before making up his mind, he had significant passages from the evening, night, and morning dialogues between Orlo and Sheeda played to him. He was not amused by the girl's 'cynicism', but after the morning interchange he had to admit that he had chosen well – as usual . . . She broke through, by God! Okay, he thought, that does it.

Continue!

Orders poured from him. Have the girl picked up, and get charges ready. Under no circumstances shall she this evening be allowed in the palace. Orlo Thomas must never see her again except on a closed circuit TV screen when she is being tortured – if that becomes necessary in order to control him. What torture? Be ready to peel off the skin of her face, as a beginning . . .

That decision made, he called Jodell and said in his mild voice, 'Prepare a plan to clean up that nest of self-serving individuals – those so-called scientists in Communications City.'

'Clean them up – when?'

'Before this day is out.'

'Does this instruction supersede your earlier caution command about doing nothing that Orlo Thomas might wonder about or be disturbed by?'

'Yes, it supersedes it – with this proviso. Have the

roundup take place during the lunch hour. I shall have Alter invite Orlo to have lunch in my apartment. From there he will at Alter's suggestion again go to visit the Gluckens, following up his promise to you yesterday that he intended to do so. This time I also want him to visit the rocket field from which the Higenroth material was launched twenty-one years ago. It should, accordingly, be quite late before he gets back – perhaps even as late as eight o'clock. Any more questions?'

'No, excellency. I think that clarifies the situation. It shall be done. Should I know where you are while your Alter is having lunch with Orlo?'

'I'll decide about that later.'

To Jodell, that meant he would not be advised. As he waited courteously for the dictator to break the connection, he presumed that Lilgin would take the opportunity to visit a neglected mistress. These were small stereotypes that he – and others – had noticed over the years. And, of course, never mentioned. He even had an idea that he knew which mistress. Odelle had recently been doing those strange things that a woman does when something is wrong . . .

What do you do on your second day of being a member of the Supreme Praesidium? Particularly, what do you do when none of your thoughts are really on your job? And when there is a terrifying sense of urgency, the need to not waste one precious minute.

Naturally, Orlo walked from his apartment to the elevator, and rode in it down to the main floor. It did not occur to him that there was anything significant about the fact that this morning he was in the elevator alone. The significance was that his absence from the leader's dinner the night before had been noticed by that group of would-be survivors. And the conclusion drawn was: don't, accidentally, get to associating with the new member until his status is further clarified. At this moment it looks like one of Lilgin's games is in progress . . . Except for Megara and Jodell, the Praesidium members were themselves too new to know what that game was.

After leaving the elevator, Orlo proceeded along the vast corridors to the guarded entrance of Communications City. From there, on being admitted, he walked to his office.

En route the same uplifting experiences as on the previous morning. Civilians bowed to him. Military personnel saluted. And when he arrived at his headquarters, there was Bylol, as obsequious as ever. And so were the members of the office staff. During his passage along the inner corridor past the separate offices, the staff people surged to their feet and did not bow. Then, a few minutes after Lidla also had bowed, and Orlo, after acknowledging, walked past her into his private office, closing the door behind him, a timid knock on that door heralded her entrance.

She walked over and stood in front of his desk. Stood there and said nothing. Waited.

Orlo was disturbed.

Am I really, seriously, going to have two women?

Unfortunately, his final parting from Sheeda had stimulated him. And – even more unfortunate – at that point she absolutely had to leave in order to go to her place of work.

Reluctantly, now, Orlo reached into a desk drawer and took out one of the pills; handed it to the girl. She swallowed it, gave him a griefy smile – and waited. Orlo gestured toward the bedroom. She ran.

He joined her there the prescribed time later. And this time, he was glad to note, they were both in better control. The day before it had been one of those wild, over-excited first times. Neither he nor she had known exactly what to do. For him, at least a part of the sad reality of *ejaculatio praecox* had dominated. And had cut short. And had embarrassed him.

This second time he remained on top of her a full five minutes; and they were both absolutely enchanted.

Afterwards, back at his desk – and Lidla back in her secretarial cubbyhole – a still guilty Orlo argued with himself that, as a consequence of what had happened, he would not disgrace himself with Sheeda that night.

Yet another thought buoyed him: the same thought as on the day before: if I'm murdered before dark, they can't take away from me that I have now, twice, had a woman. (And Lidla a man.)

That seemed very real, and meaningful. And not at all naive.

Imagine, if he had lived nearly twenty-one years. And

then died without that. And Lidla the same – for obviously he was her only option.

Somehow, that transcended the curious loyalty he was beginning to feel toward Sheeda, as if she had some special right with him. His obligation to Sheeda (he argued silently) was to make sure that she, also, did not die without having fulfilled herself as a woman.

That (grimly) is one of the true realities of Lilgin-land.

He felt guilty for another reason. The episode with Lidla had taken up nearly forty minutes . . . all that preliminary kissing and petting.

We who are somehow being used by the dictator, and – somehow – hoping to take advantage of that . . . had better get on with the job.

Doing what? he wondered.

Sitting there, he wrote a mental essay:

'I, Orlo Thomas, a nobody who has been making tiny but secret rebel noises since the age of eleven – but for the most part haven't worked very hard at it – a short time ago was motivated to make my rebel stand.

'Instead of promptly having charges placed against me, I was brought to the palace of the dictator, and promoted to be one of the thirty or so most powerful men in the world.

'It is my presumptuous belief that this dictator is an immortal man – which is pretty ridiculous (yet otherwise certain enduring consistencies of government cannot be explained) – and that he has an as yet unknown – to me – purpose for bringing me here to the heartland of power on this planet.

'If this last is true, the question becomes: does anyone else know what that purpose is? If not, obviously then except for a few imprisoned scientists, I'm in this alone; and am probably going to die without ever knowing the facts.

'BUT – if someone else is aware of Lilgin's purpose with me, then my theory that millions of people everywhere are waiting for an opportunity to break the power of this super-villain of all earth history, could extend (I hope) even here to the palace.

'What purpose could said dictator have with me that would justify even one person risking his own skin? . . .'

Having 'written' the little summary on a sort of a

blackboard of the mind, Orlo 'stared' gloomily at the final paragraph.

Really, he thought, I'm out of my mind to even imagine such madness . . . The summary was true, word for word, and in a logical world had to have some explanation, but —

His thought was torn from its track.

The door to his office just about burst off its hinges.

Bylol darted in. His eyes were wide, and almost blank. He blurted, 'His excellency is on the phone.'

'Lilgin?'

Having spoken, Orlo became almost as blank as the other man. Presumably, he got a yes, or a nod. But it didn't register, whatever it was.

When the blankness ended, Orlo thought shakily: after all, I talked to him two evenings ago. On the surface, he isn't that hard to talk to . . .

But the inner tremor was still there as he reached for the receiver. Lifting it automatically turned on the viewplate. And there was the famous face.

'Mr. Thomas,' said the familiar, resonant voice, 'will you have lunch with me in my apartment today?'

'Yes, *sir*,' said Orlo. 'What time?'

'Twelve-thirty. D-One. The guards will have orders to admit you, so just walk in.'

After the contact was broken, Orlo glanced limply at his watch: Eleven minutes after ten. He had come in shortly after nine.

The day was barely begun.

When he looked up after thinking about that, Bylol had disappeared.

He sagged back into his chair. Inside him, a single word used by the dictator was making an impact: '. . . the guards . . .'

He thought, gulping: how to disappear in one easy lesson? Have lunch with Martin Lilgin . . .

Suddenly, he needed advice badly.

Up he swayed. Out of his back door he hurried. Out in the corridor he grew calm. Grew thoughtful.

Grew brave.

He thought: once more the intent is to draw me away from the scientists' luncheon. This time using total power.

Why? . . . For God's sake, what is this?

He found Ishkrin in the library, reading. The two men located McIntosh, and then, with relief, ran into Arger of the magic ability to protect against spies. And, since the rapid minutes had already flown, settled for that much of a group.

Orlo wrote: I have an awful feeling that my coming to yesterday's luncheon has endangered all the men in Communications City.

His reasoning: By bringing into the open that the scientists did not intend to do anything about the Higenroth project, he had possibly triggered in the dictator's mind one of the sweeping, destructive thoughts which in times past had caused entire groups and areas to be decimated.

The anger that he envisaged was: They're in Communications City for one purpose, and if they don't accept that's what they're there for, strike them from the face of the earth!

Within the frame of the triple-level conversation – written, bugged, and unbugged – the great grey moustache of Ishkrin moved up, and down, and sideways, and the friendly voice or pen conveyed . . . unconcern.

'We're all doomed men,' he said. 'As individuals, at the doom moment we're all prepared to take with us one or more of the persons sent against us. But since they'll only be dupes themselves, it could be that some of us will not even exercise that privilege.'

Having spoken, his grey eyes stared blandly into Orlo's blue ones.

And Orlo got the message. These men still didn't trust him. Because what he was doing now, and what he had done late yesterday evening, could be a come-on game that he was trying to work on them. His charging out here to look for them so that he could sound an alarm, from one point of view had the look of a tactic.

It was stalemate forever. 'Okay,' he said, resigned. 'I trust you know what you're doing.'

'If,' said Ishkrin without flinching, 'you had behind you our long years in this endless nightmare, and if we knew what your role is, and what Lilgin has in mind for you – I might be able to give you some other answer. Failing that –' he shrugged, and smiled '– have a pleasant luncheon with Chairman Lilgin, Orlo.'

On his way back to his office, Orlo thought: what other answer could he give me? . . .

It was amazing. In those final, denying words, he had in effect received the other answer:

If necessary, in a crisis, the scientists *could* act.

NINETEEN

Except for guard barriers, the corridor that stretched away from the open elevator door was the same as farther down.

Orlo stepped out onto the fourth floor, then paused to evaluate the barriers.

The first one was a steel fence which stretched from the inner wall to within a few feet of the plate window. It was at least seven feet high; and the long table behind it must have been on a raised dais. For the dozen youths who sat at the table peered over at him.

Orlo remembered his instructions, and walked slowly forward. The youths looked at him, but said nothing. He walked through the gap between the window and the fence. They let him.

Ahead was a second steel fence. This one stretched from the plate glass to within a yard of the inner wall. The same kind of young heads were visible behind it.

They, also, let him pass. Silently. Without a word. Stony-faced.

Orlo did not look back at either group to verify if they were in uniform, or if they were in fact sitting at a high desk. (They could all be eight feet tall, and standing.)

Ahead was a third barrier. Different. Not metal – and no guards. At least none visible. What it was was a sort of an arbor. Ornate. Flowers grew cunningly out of the floor, and up a trellis. And on the floor, a carpet pathway in red and blue and yellow – the personal colours of Martin Lilgin.

The entire attempt at an appearance of outdoors pointed slantingly at a wide, gilt door. Orlo walked up to that door, checked to make sure if it was in fact, D-One. Whereupon, bracing himself, he did as he had been told: fingered the latch, opened the door, stepped inside, and closed the door behind him.

. . . The two men – the little Lilgin and the medium Orlo – sat in a gleaming glass room at a glass table, and ate from and with crystal and silver dishes and silver cutlery.

During the meal, Orlo acknowledged the instructions he was given: First, re-visit the Gluckens . . .

On that, his host smiled, and said gently, 'Jodell and I shall look forward with interest to the results of such a second interrogation. And perhaps even a third one to-morrow. It's astonishing, sometimes, what a new mind can discover from old material . . .' So, glibly, stated the false Lilgin, pursuant to his instructions.

The Alter also 'advised' the visit to the rocket-field. And, of course, Orlo had no alternative but to say that he would go there after his visit to the Gluckens.

Finally, they were at coffee and dessert. At which time the obsequious waiters disappeared.

Whereupon, Lilgin promptly took two sheets of paper from an inner pocket, unfolded them, and handed them to Orlo. The totally surprised Orlo read:

'Keep reading this even if I continue talking. This may be my single opportunity, ever, to tell you that I am only the Alter Ego of Chairman Lilgin. Which means that I attend functions, and even important meetings, as if I am he.

'My first thought to you is: Since the instructions about your afternoon and evening activities came to me from Lilgin himself, you must of course obey them.

'But, now, hear this:

'I have become convinced that I am about to be killed. I replaced somebody who disappeared a few years ago. And it is obvious that you represent a crisis of such severity that no one who knows anything about it can be permitted to live when it is over.

'I am a person who fits in that category. I know too much, or, at least, a lot. A substitute for a major leader has to be well-briefed on numerous sensitive subjects. And while I have never been taken aside and briefed about you directly, the details have been coming through.

'What I have gathered is that you are the son of Martin Lilgin by one of his mistresses of twenty or so years ago. The problem for you derives from the fact that Jodell and Megara want to start the long process of getting you ready to become Lilgin's heir and successor when he dies – he is actually older than he looks; well into his fifties.

'However, Lilgin is an egotist; and is not really interested in having an heir named. In fact, being paranoid, he has somehow got the idea that a complex plot, revolving around you, is being mounted against him. In the past whenever he has been confronted by something he doesn't understand, or fears, his method has been to kill. Would a man, you may ask, kill his own son? I have to tell you that fully half of Lilgin's own relatives are either in prison, or executed; so the answer is yes.

'His decision is that you will be put out of the way – soon. The exact date is not clear to me. But it could even be tomorrow.

'Now what this means is we must act swiftly. My suggestion is that I immediately – within twenty-four hours – assassinate Chairman Martin Lilgin – and that I then step into his shoes. Where I need your backing for that is that you must help me carry through this pretence by giving me full and continuous recognition. I've been practising his handwriting; so I'm sure I can pass. As soon as I'm established, I shall declare you to be my heir. That will win the support of Megara and Jodell, the two most powerful men after Lilgin himself. We can all go on then as if nothing has happened except the death of what seems to be a nonentity, that is, an Alter Ego.

'What do you think? Will you go along with that?'

What Orlo was thinking by the time he reached the final words was that now he could understand the feelings of the scientists when he had asked for their help.

They had felt that they couldn't trust Orlo Thomas. And now his mind was a veritable hodgepodge of conflicting impulses, which, after a minute, coalesced into a single Great Big Doubt.

The story did not sound absolutely implausible to him.

It provided a farfetched, but not entirely incredible, explanation for why he had been made a member of the Supreme Praesidium of earth. (There had to be a logical reason. *Had to be.*)

But the whole notion of engaging in a conspiracy to

murder the dictator, was beyond his immediate reality. And what was worse, he was being asked to agree to cooperate in such a crime with a man who might be Lilgin himself.

. . . Too much.

Belatedly, he remembered how Ishkrin had handled a similar dilemma only an hour or so earlier.

He said carefully, 'I should say that I am greatly bewildered by everything that has happened to me in the past few days. Throughout, my goal is to remain on the winner's side, and to stay alive, if I can . . .'

Later, on the jet flight to the Gluckens, Orlo thought, shuddering: – that I got away at all suggests that maybe he was the Alter Ego . . .

What bothered him was, if the story was true – what then?

. . . The story was thoroughly believed by the deluded Alter. In his time he had been accurately briefed on many major aspects of government. He could see no reason why this was different.

However, this was. This required misleading statements. And that was exactly what the dictator had done to his little Alter: misled him. Casual remarks made in passing. An attitude which implied that the Alter was one of the insiders, though the matter (it was suggested) did not strongly concern him. The dinner that first evening. And now the luncheon. Simple.

Chairman Lilgin had always operated on three principles: where it doesn't matter, tell the exact truth in tiresome detail – that was number one. Principle Two was: never give information on anything important until it becomes necessary to do so. Three: whenever possible keep your enemies, or potential enemies, confused.

An exceedingly confused Orlo went off on his two meaningless errands. The private schemes and fears of the Alter Ego had, in effect, demolished all his own theories.

He arrived back at the palace when it was already dark, feeling foolish, disturbed, unhappy, bewildered, torn. And his only good thought was that Sheeda would be waiting for him.

There was a vague impulse in him to seek out Ishkrin again. But his spirit had been diminished by the events of the day. So that remained vague.

As a result of that abdication of responsibility, he did not learn of the battle in Communications City between the scientists and the palace guards. Not that he would have been permitted to go into that shambles. Lilgin had given strict orders to bar him. Nevertheless, everyone was relieved when he did not even try.

Such things, of course, were not entirely without value. By being tired, he avoided an evening confrontation – which might have led to unknown reactions. Yet his avoidance raised a question: Can a twenty-one-year-old save himself in a complex plot? For the Orlo who walked wearily into his apartment, the answer was at least temporarily no.

The clobbering thought was an immensely simple one: – if I am really the son of Martin Lilgin, obviously I can personally do nothing against him . . .

By midnight, when there was still no sign nor sound of Sheeda, he was lying fully dressed on the bed, miserable, hopeless, exhausted, and confused.

Presently, he slipped into a depth of sleep that bordered on unconsciousness.

TWENTY

Long ago, the experts had decided that there were specific biorythms around which, into which, at which Higenroth must have projected his programming of the (then) newly joined sperm and ovum that would eventually become a baby, a child, a youth.

They were not concerned with the man. It was tacitly realized by all the undersucklings that there would never be a fully mature Higenroth issue.

An accelerated study of what was already known about biorythms – which was a lot – received, of course, all the computer time requested.

Final summing up: The third of three programmings will take effect between 5.10 A.M. and 7.04 A.M. on the day of the 21st birthday. The first two took effect at age eleven and age fifteen, respectively.

Naturally, all the people involved in the inquiry subsequently had charges placed against them. The dictator was particularly happy to be able to dispose of the investigating group because that final report spread the time over a two hour period.

The failure of the Committee's members to pinpoint the exact moment, incensed him.

The charges were: serious errors, defects in their work, suspicion of volunteerism.

After that, nothing could save them. They disappeared forever a short time later.

The errors they had made were, in fact, more serious, even, than the charges indicated. When Orlo was eleven – and later when he was fifteen – he was questioned as to the origin of certain thoughts he had (the Higenroth programming for those ages, correctly observed for what it was).

Since the questioning method seemed to be a part of the confessional style brainwashing that was periodically required of everyone, Orlo reported accurately. At which time it was observed that the thoughts were initially present in a shadowy form approximately two hours before they suddenly came through crystal-clear.

The two hour (less a few minutes) period confused the observers.

Worse, they had missed the real cue a full seventy-two hours earlier; which was not a thought but an overstimulated body feeling. Unforgivably, they had not noticed the even more distant-in-time cue six weeks before that.

Because everything about the mind is complex – but there is a structure, there is a mechanism – at least two physical-mental factors were involved. One was in the brain itself: an actual neutral function that scans upcoming associations in advance. Thus, a person trying to remember a name has that name available approximately two hours before it finally surfaces. It is not available in that earlier time as an exact memory; but he will have a physiologic association that relates to the person whose name he is trying to recall.

The second factor, in this instance, was of course the Higenroth programming. Six weeks in advance, anger and resistance; seventy-two hours in advance, the entire glandular system stimulated: the body mobilized for action. People in this condition, even if they have not previously exercised, can run up hills; their eyes shine, their step is springy, their mind bright. Such a person glitters. At the scientists' luncheon that first day, Orlo had glittered in this fantastic fashion, astounding everybody there. (Once people have been brought up to this condition, they never quite lose it.)

The Committee, like its master, had been so paranoid throughout that it did not notice that in between ages eleven and fifteen, and fifteen and twenty-one (minus six weeks), Orlo was essentially peaceful and conformist. Like the Great Big – but physically little – Genius, the members of the Committee assumed what was called 'omnipresence of disguised enemies'; who knew at all times what they were doing, and were in some manner doing it all the time.

Naturally, during the in-between times, Orlo remembered the thoughts he had had during the key moments. But he had been told that the system of self-criticism freed a person from ideas inimical To The People; and he believed that. So between eleven and fifteen he quickly put 'old-style' ideas out of the forefront of his mind and was properly ashamed of himself. That was harder to do after age fifteen, but essentially his 'rightist exaggeration' concentrated on how to avoid being a teenage dupe.

Orlo awakened in darkness, and lay still; not quite awake – Did I have a dream? Or did I hear a sound? . . .

There was a movement in the dark near the bed. Whoever it was seemed to have a sure awareness of where he was. There was a flicker of shadow against shadow; and then a strong hand clamped over his mouth, and another hand grabbed his mouth, and pressed.

If he had any consciousness after that, Orlo did not remember it afterwards.

Blackness.

When he came to, he was lying – still fully dressed – on a couch in his office.

Orlo blinked, as he realized it was broad daylight. And realized where he was.

He sat up – and saw . . . fantasia.

On every plastic wall, and on all the glass surfaces, there were pictures of a live Martin Lilgin

TWENTY-ONE

Is there a special shock that a super-dictator feels when he is finally brought to bay? Does he change colour? And get that sickening crunch sensation inside?

Can it be that the Big Fear strikes? And in that intense moment is there actually the thought: They got me!

And what about disbelief – could that be in him? The incredible! The blank thought that this can't be happening to me! Not *me*.

Surely, such a man must have in him some of the utter madness of the old divine right of kings; the conviction that he is special, and that, somehow, all this power he has had was bestowed on him for a purpose, but basically because he is who he is.

Nobody would ever know. On the plastic wall that Orlo watched first, it was already evident that Lilgin had been aware for some time of his situation. And had made at least an initial adjustment.

He was smiling faintly. He hummed a little as he shaved. He completed dressing.

Then he went down to his office, and sat at the famous desk. It was there that he had breakfast brought to him. And later lunch. And dinner.

The desk! It was famous because this was where television cameras found him on those rare occasions when he spoke to the world. There he would be sitting, with papers piled to his right, and papers to his left. And as the camera dollied in, he would look up with that distracted expression of a man who has too many things to do, but is doggedly doing them.

This time, after he had seated himself, he said, 'I shall make a statement at 10 o'clock, eastern standard time. Until then, I'll be busy with all this.' He smiled, and indicated the stacks of documents.

Whereupon, he took the top paper from the nearest pile, scanned through it, called his secretary – who was sitting almost petrified off to one side – and dictated a letter. The secretary (a young male) seemed to be having difficulties.

But Lilgin paid no attention, though he did make the letter brief . . . something about a change in procedure at a collective farm.

He sent the man away with the instruction to transmit the letter at once. Then he began to read the documents. And a little later breakfast was brought; and he ate and read sort of like a person who takes his newspaper to his meal; and combines the two: the impression of a busy man who cannot take time off for routine activities.

At ten o'clock, he looked up with a smile, and made a brief statement:

'Comrades, workers, supporters of the New Economic System. I imagine that you were all surprised this morning when you saw my image on one or another wall in your house. I have been persuaded, partly against my better judgement – but not entirely – to make a test of indeterminate duration, meaning (smile) we don't know how long the test will go on. The idea is this: that the citizens and comrades and workers have a right to keep an eye on their government. There are always rumours that secret activities are going on at high government levels, that actions are taken which are not made public. Etc. etc. etc. – you know these things. You've heard about them from many sources. Some of these sources are merely unknowing people – which is most of the population of this planet: hardworking, loyal, law-abiding, eager to improve working conditions. Other sources of such rumours are not that reliable. They have ulterior motives; and so once in a while they become difficult and the security forces have to deal with them according to laws which can be examined at any public library. In any event, with this marvellous invention, we are now in a position – so I am told – to make a test that will give everyone an opportunity to judge for himself if he wants to see the process of government at close range hour after hour, day after day. While this test is in progress, logic requires that it will continue both day and night. I hope that you won't mind if I turn out the lights when I undress, and that I go to the bathroom in pitch darkness. My suggestion is that as a courtesy to me you yourself do not watch me at all at such times. That completes my report for the time being. When I am ready to make another one, I shall announce it in advance, also. Thank you – and I cannot say good day, because, as you will see, I will not be leaving. So perhaps I'd better say, Ladies and gentlemen, keep your eye on the government. Here is your chance to learn all the drab, dreary details that pass across my desk year in and year out. I can tell you right now it isn't very exciting. But it is necessary, and it is worthwhile.'

That was the completion. The famous face remained with its smile on it for several seconds longer. Then the hand waved a final greeting, at which point the head bent; and the eyes began to scan another document.

The appearance was that Martin Lilgin, dictator of earth, had returned to his many duties.

Orlo had come to, feeling groggy. He sat up when the speech began. He listened to it, confused, not knowing what to make of it, with no awareness of direct involvement.

When it was over, he hurried out of his private entrance; headed toward the residence part of Communications City – and, after a little, as he rounded one of those great marble-walled corridor bends, came to a barrier guarded by scientists.

One of the men at the barrier was from table Seven – the Chinese astronomer, Jimmy Ho.

Jimmy cautioned, 'Don't come any closer, Orlo!'

Orlo was flabbergasted. But he stopped. 'What's going on? What's happening?'

It took a small mountain of dialogue to straighten that out. Finally, anxiously: 'Was anybody killed?'

'Some of those poor kids in uniform. They came trooping into the commissary yesterday lunch time, and made a big display of guns and toughness. So we just had to prove right there that nobody comes into certain parts of Communications City unless we're willing to have him as a guest. I understand there's only two days' food in the freezers. So that puts the time limit on how long we can hold out – maybe a week.'

'Don't be ridiculous!' said Orlo. 'All this must be a mistake. After all, I'm in charge here, legally. So whoever gave the order did so without proper legality. We've got to establish realities like that.'

'Dream on, fella!' said Jimmy Ho. But he remained cheerful.

Orlo said urgently, 'Will you find Ishkrin, and ask him to

bring to my office a couple of experts on what's happening. I'd like to talk to somebody about –' He gestured with both arms, indicating the walls. The images were dimmer on the marble surface; but it was possible to see the flicker of them on particularly shiny surfaces '– about this. Tell him to bring along an explanation of why direction finders don't seem to have spotted the source in – what was it he said? – three seconds.'

The round, smooth, Chinese face was grinning. 'He was just pulling your funny bone, Orlo. The word, pervasive, means that the source is just part of the whole. It's neither visible, audible, nor detectable. This thing can go on until the machinery out there breaks down; and I'm willing to bet that Higenroth equipment has got plenty of backup to keep it going for a while – like maybe a hundred years.'

Orlo uttered an awed, 'Good God!' And had the feeling of growing excitement as he headed back to his office. Another thought he had was: what fantastic good luck I'm having, being here when someone finally got that Higenroth thing going. And to think I only heard about him, or it, a couple of days ago . . .

Back at his desk, conscious that the dancing feeling was again pulsating inside him, he rang for Bylol.

Waiting, he consciously considered his own situation.

There were still problems, and the fantastic mystery of what had happened to him in the night. But he had none of the confusion of the afternoon, evening, and night before.

Sitting there, waiting, he glittered again.

TWENTY-TWO

The worms were crawling out of the woodwork. And they had rows of spikes sticking out of their minds, and they were filled with bitter juices.

A substantial while after Orlo rang, Mr. Bylol entered. There were changes in his manner. He walked in; he didn't run. He'll probably get fat now, Orlo thought cynically, as he gazed up at the gaunt individual.

A moment of amazement, then. He was, he realized,

seeing the man for the very first time, really. Until this instant his impression had been that Bylol was a gangling, dried-up oldish man.

The rehabilitated Chief Assistant to the Praesidium Member in charge of science and technology, who strolled through the door, looked to be in his late thirties. As the mildly insolent Bylol sauntered over to Orlo's desk, he said casually, 'I was on the phone when you called. The call is for you. Three - pardon me! - Mr. Jodell is waiting on your intercom.'

Orlo, who had reached into the pocket where the gun was at the instant Bylol entered, kept his hand on the weapon. He did not genuinely believe that this man was capable of violent or decisive action. But this thought was: take no chances.

'Thank you, Mr. Bylol.' He spoke courteously. 'What do you think of this experiment that Chairman Lilgin has undertaken?'

There was a pause. The man's eyes changed first . . . Nothing, analyzed Orlo, like persuading someone to speak his thoughts, so that he can see what they are -

'Uh!' gurgled Mr. Bylol. It was almost then as if he plopped back from another dimension. '*Sir*, Mr. Jodell is on the intercom,' he said. And it was the old-style over-stimulated tone.

With that said, he backed out, bowing and scraping, and did it on the double.

Orlo picked up the intercom receiver. 'Sorry to keep you waiting, sir,' he lied. 'I was in the bathroom.'

The jovial being at the other end of the line cut him off. 'Don't give it a thought, my young friend. I wonder if I could come over and talk to you?'

Orlo said, 'How old are you, Mr. Jodell? You look about fifty-five.'

The two men were sitting across Orlo's desk from each other. And from the first moment it was straight talk, as if Three had decided to burn his past - and, if necessary, his future; and didn't care who heard what.

The heavy jowls changed colour now from a kind of purple to pink rage. The steely eyes narrowed. 'That S.O.B.,' he said venomously, 'keeps Megara and me looking, and feeling, an old middle fifties, and himself a young forty.' He seemed to realize that he was being subjective. He straightened a little. 'I'm two hundred and twenty-seven years old,' he said proudly. 'And I suppose I ought to be greateful to that so-and-so; but I had to earn every year of it. So to hell with him!'

'Would you like to tell me the story?'

Jodell nodded, and a tear sprang into each eye. 'It's been building up in me for a hundred and seventy-five years, and I've reached the point where I want to tell it to little boys, or even to friendly rocks.'

'Keep going,' said Orlo.

Number Three was a survivor.

Formerly an equal, he had managed to make the transition to subordinate. Which had not been easy to do. The term for people like him in the deadly days following the takeover had been either left deviationist or right deviationist.

The sentence was always death.

A deviationist was a man who, in the early days, had lacked a specific type of E.S.P. Somehow or other he had failed to notice that a certain, small, dark-haired, wolfish young man with jet black eyes was *the* natural leader of the new-forming world-state.

He might argue, as many did, that there were so many things on his mind, including self-seeking, that he had neglected to be aware that a transition state had its natural leader. And he had simply not realized for a dangerously long time that there was only one possible choice of who that leader should be.

Fortunately for Jodell he had never, actually, at group meetings found fault with the dark-haired, coyote-like being. Most of the top echelon people had. They were all dead as dead could be shortly thereafter.

But that alone – not having criticized – couldn't have saved anyone. His good fortune transcended anything as simplistic as that. The truth was that all of the old people constituted what was subsequently called a Negative Group.

They had committed an unforgivable, though inadvertent, crime. They had been present at the creation. No matter how you demote such a man, or to what distant nothing task you assign him, he remembers things about you. He knew you when. Somewhere in his head is an awareness that you, also, are a human being with human faults.

He saw you accused of making errors. And saw you defend yourself like any ordinary human being. He was there on the day that a Party Member (long dead now, tortured for days, and arguing incredulously every minute, screaming until almost the instant of death against your right to do this before finally accepting that this *was* happening, and that there was nobody out there to stop it, because they also were being tortured and murdered at the same time) had said that you, Martin Lilgin, were an extreme left deviate with fascist orientation.

Can a man be allowed to live who has heard such a charge made against that certain, small, hyenaish leader? He can if he was the first to take pen in hand – except for Megara, he was the first – and write, stating that he recognized the superman with the cobra eyes and instincts as his natural superior for all future time in the newly-formed world state. He can if that ultra-leader has tentatively decided that he will permit approximately one hundred of the original eight or so million to remain alive; and has no fixed idea as to precisely who those hundred shall be. Each man will have to win his own place in that select coterie by some unique act of obeisance.

Part of the requirement turned out to be that each of the hundred shall be noted for his perfect memory of how in the early days everything that the leader did was right; and that he was, in fact, never wrong about anything.

Each of the hundred – it turned out – uniformly recalled every single event leading up to the victory. And was prepared to testify – and did so testify repeatedly – that one and only one person played the decisive role in every instance. And that no one else did anything except obey orders . . .

'What,' asked Orlo, 'was the name of the inventor of the immortality pill?'

They had reached the stage of question and answer.

Jodell said, 'We don't know yet if it will produce immortality. But it's good enough.' He shrugged, and added simply, 'One morning I woke up, and I couldn't remember either the fellow's name or what I had done with the formula. I don't know how Lilgin did that.'

'There would have been a discussion about those exact items,' said systems engineer (of a sort) Orlo Thomas, 'and simultaneously you would have been breathing –' he named a gas derivative of a chemical compound related to sodium pentathol '– or else had it injected into your blood stream in some other way.'

'I don't remember such a conversation,' said Jodell.

'It would be a little difficult,' Orlo commented drily, 'with such a method.'

He was briefly silent, visualizing this new piece of information, seeing those actions in a series of shadowy mental images. Presumably, the discoverer of immortality was, himself, long dead. Stripped of his brainchild while he was still alive. Skilfully manoeuvred – probably for years – into an unwary release of the data. Logic said that he was kept around until it was established beyond all question that the secret formula could be manufactured, and injected, without his assistance; until finally it reposed in one of the dictator's hiding places.

It could even be that, while he was alive, the inventor had been a member of the Supreme Praesidium. Orlo asked the question. And in reply got a shrug. 'There were so many,' said Jodell, sounding helpless.

'I know,' said Orlo, who was probably the only person who had ever counted them.

At this point, Orlo could restrain himself no longer. The tension had been building up in him from the moment of Jodell's phone call: the feeling that both the phone conversation and this dialogue had been, and were being, monitored; and that someone had the authority to act against traitors. For some reason, Jodell's total ignoring of the disastrous possibilities had kept Orlo silent, also. It was as if his bravery had to match the older man's.

But, now, he asked *that* question.

Jodell said, surprised, 'For Pete's sake, Orlo, Lilgin has only got twenty-four hours like the rest of us. Spying on you and your equipment was my job. And –' grim smile '–the purpose, after all, was to prevent you from doing what has now been done, and was designed to obtain that invention, also.'

'What you're saying,' persisted Orlo, 'is that, since spying on me was your job, this conversation has not been, and is not being, monitored by anyone. Is that correct?'

Jodell was apologetic. 'I should have mentioned that right away. Yes, yes, that's it, of course. What else.' He leaned back. The jovial expression was back on his face. 'All right, now tell me how you did it?'

'Did what?' Blankly.

'Come, come –' There was instant power and impatience in that voice, so accustomed was it to giving orders and dealing with subordinates '– how did you locate that S.O.B.? I tell you he never intended for you to get so much as a glimpse of him. And it's possible that, except for Megara, I was the only one who had all that subtle information that made it possible for me – and, naturally, Megara – to guess that Chairman Lilgin spent the afternoon, evening, and night with Odette.'

'I,' said Orlo in an even voice, 'haven't the faintest idea what you're talking about. Now, you've made a couple of comments earlier that puzzled me when you said them – and still puzzle me. But I let them slide by. So the first thing we've got to clarify is, what the hell are you talking about?'

There was a long pause, and dead silence. Finally, Jodell said quietly, 'Higenroth. You're Higenroth's son. And all this –' He did the waving motion at the images '– is coming out of your head.'

'But,' Orlo said, weakly, 'the Alter Ego told me yesterday that I was Lilgin's son.'

'He never was too bright,' said Jodell. 'And if that's a sample of his reasoning, you can see why Lilgin had him killed yesterday afternoon, as soon as you and he had lunch, and you were gone.'

'He was going to be the new dictator,' said Orlo, 'and make me his heir.'

'Quite a few Alters have had that thought,' said Jodell in a dismissing tone. 'But now, listen, what –'

'Higenroth's son!' mused Orlo aloud.

Oddly, he was not too happy about it. In fact, it almost seemed like a comedown. He found himself wryly recalling reading about an earlier dictator named Adolf Hitler, who, it had developed, was really Adolf Schickelgruber. The name, Higenroth, had something of the Schickelgruber in it. He tried it in a whisper: 'Orlo Higenroth.' Ugh!

A hand reached across the desk at that moment, and grasped his wrist. 'Where are you?' said Jodell, firmly. 'You seem to have disappeared.'

Orlo explained, unhappily, about the Orlo Schickelgruber thing. 'I feel demoted.'

'Greatest communications genius who ever lived. He was psyched out by the teenage girl Lilgin married him to. We discovered later that she had locked the bedroom door. So the only time she lay down for him was on the eve of his death, when she was scared out of her mind. And that, my young friend –' Jodell smiled grimly '– is how you came to be the repository of the secret of the Pervasive System, which, you now tell me, you have no recollection of using against Lilgin.'

Thus, abruptly, they were back to that.

Orlo said, 'When you called, I took it for granted that it was you who had me transported from my bedroom to this office.'

'Not me,' said Jodell in a strained voice.

The youth and the man stared at each other. And presently, as if moved by the same string, climbed to their feet.

'But – but –' blurted Orlo.

Jodell held out a hand that shook slightly. 'Let me have that 'com,' he said hoarsely.

Silently, Orlo pushed the instrument across the desk. He watched as an intent Three fingered two studs, paused, then touched two more.

The face that came on the plate was of a man of Jodell's age. Orlo had seen him at the dinner that first night – another of the drunkards.

Megara!

Jodell said, 'Veet, I'm here in Orlo Thomas's office. And we've just come to an astounding conclusion. You did it.'

The face on the plate was one of those grown-up baby faces, with a little moustache on the upper lip, and small blueish eyes. Except for the jaw it was a face that – Orlo wouldn't have been surprised – could burst into tears on a moment's notice. But apparently even babies can get tough after two hundred and twenty years.

This face broke into a faint smile. Then the deep un-babyish voice said, 'Opportunities like Orlo come along only once in even a long lifetime. I can tell you it was a pleasure to finally get that bastard.'

He broke off. 'But, listen, I'd better get over there. We've got to remember that Lilgin is also thinking hard. And he doesn't have to utter a death sentence aloud; he can just write them out in his own handwriting. My suggestion is that I become the head of government. Think about that while you're waiting, will you?'

After the connection was broken, Jodell commented cynically, 'I see there are plenty of willing replacements. And there will be more with the same thoughts. Including, possibly, even me. And –' with a smile '– you.'

'Not me,' said Orlo.

TWENTY-THREE

He could perceive . . . signals.

A trusted aide could utter one wrong word – and he never got another chance to speak. A politically correct statement spoken with the tiniest lapse from correct tone of voice – Lilgin heard the lapse. That man was not allowed near him again.

And, of course, in due – but rapid – course, both men disappeared after first being tortured by the fatigue method into making a 'full confession'.

Signals! In the days long ago, when he was in his teens, and when there were still private automobiles, the faintest signal of malfunction in the machine had alerted that youthful Martin Lilgin. His car was in the garage so often, beginning on the day of his taking delivery, that mechanics groaned the instant they saw him drive up.

It did not dawn on either the young, or the maturing, Lilgin, or on his subsequent supporters (all presently murdered) that extreme, untrained sensitivity to signals is abnormal. He admired himself for that; considered it precocious of himself; and so did many persons who later projected that one deadly (for themselves) signal that advised The Boss that they had had a thought of their own . . . critical.

Abnormal sensitivity to signals (in the paranoid way) is a physiologic condition of the second stage of fatigue. Since Lilgin had never to his knowledge been subjected to unusual fatigue, and of course did not consider what he did as paranoid, it did not occur to him (at least, he would not entertain the possibility) that the body can experience certain illnesses like sustained high fever, which duplicate on a deep cellular and neural level those first two stages of fatigue, and sometimes even the third.

As a baby (so his mother had once told him) he was fever-sick almost unto death. In his subsequent great days, he monitored the information from her telling, and transformed it into a system: *all* fever illnesses must be recorded, and the people and their subsequent behaviour followed up. For some reason, he restrained himself from using that particular data to motivate mass murder of the persons who were thus named. Perhaps, to do that would have been like judging himself, also.

Shortly after making his speech on that first day of total communication, he had 'listened' to all the signals of his predicament.

At that point, he asked for a quire of official form Ten-Sixties to be brought to him. His secretary charged out of the room, and came back with a message from Jodell that the stationery supply office (which for that form was located in Jodell's department) was fresh out. But that the forms were being printed up.

As a substitute for the official death order forms, the secretary brought along two quires of blank sheets. He placed them on Lilgin's desk. And retreated into the background. The dictator had the impression – the signal came to him – that the man was hiding a smile. In front of three billion people, Lilgin had to suppress his instant impulse to have the rascal struck dead.

All these people in the palace, he thought, who have seen me in this state of degradation, will have to go . . .

Death of all such memories!

The thought calmed him, as he sat there. For it kind of said in advance that what was happening was not really being witnessed.

But actually his mind was made up.

What to do.

Deliberately, he broke open one of the quires. Drew out a stack of sheets. And began to write death sentences in his own handwriting. He folded each one personally; and placed it in an envelope, and sealed and addressed the envelope.

When he had done this half a dozen times, he looked up with his smile, and said to the watching billions. 'At four P.M., I shall explain what I am doing, and why.'

'What do you think he's writing?' asked Ishkrin.

The question, presumably, was addressed to all seven of the men who sat in Orlo's office – and even, perhaps, to himself, the eighth.

Orlo answered first. 'Hmmm –' he leaned back with a frown '– I suppose I should be analyzing that.' He closed his eyes.

'Do you think,' Ishkrin continued, 'he's finally decided whether this is a right or left deviationist plot?'

All the scientists in the room smiled with their timeless good humour. Megara and Jodell sat sombre, and silent.

Orlo opened his eyes and said, 'I think Praesidium Members Numbers Two and Three should have their girl friends or wives brought to this section within the next hour – and that reminds me.' He sat up, and leaned forward across the desk toward Jodell. 'Where's Sheeda?'

Without waiting, he thereupon shoved the intercom across the desk once more. Jodell accepted the instrument. His stubby fingers flicked over the studs.

A hard face came onto the 'com plate. It was young, square, grim. It listened to the older man's question. Then the mouth opened; and the voice that issued from it, said, 'I have a written order here in the handwriting of Chairman Martin Lilgin, ordering me to hold onto Sheeda Moorton, and to be ready to tear her to shreds on the shredding machine on the receipt of a single word over the 'com from him.'

'Is that order written on a Ten-Sixty form?' asked Jodell in his most even voice.

'No, but the handwriting is well-known to me.'

'I'm sure –' wryly '– it is. But now listen, Bureski, we

want that girl. Never mind the order. These are changing times, and you must change with them.'

The grim voice said, 'What the hell is going on over there? What is this test?'

'It's no test, my friend. He's been caught at last. And there's nothing he or anyone else can do. So don't get caught with him. We're going to send somebody over to pick up that girl.'

'Impossible. I may not obey the order, as given here. But I will not hand her over, or release her at this time.'

Jodell glanced over at the scientists. 'Gentlemen, I'm going to make a threat on your behalf. Listen to it, and tell me if you can carry it through.' He turned back to the viewplate. He said, 'Bureski, I'm sending half a dozen scientists from Communications City to that dark grey Secret Police headquarters of yours. And they will come in and get the girl. Don't resist! Hand her over.'

The square face was incredulous. 'Half a dozen –' he yelped. 'Why, we're a fortress here. We're even equipped to shoot down atomic missiles.'

'This is a case of mind over matter,' said Jodell drily. He glanced at Ishkrin. 'Have I stated the situation correctly?'

'It will require about a dozen interacting specialists,' was the reply. 'Maybe even only ten.'

'Good,' said Jodell. 'And now, Bureski, don't go away. We also want to locate Madame Megara –'

Over in the corner settee, there was a strange, harsh sound from Megara. It was very much the sound of a grown man from whom has been evoked a surprised cry of grief.

After Jodell had broken the connection, he said to no one in particular, 'Just in case anybody's wondering, I can probably in an emergency arrange for all of us to escape to The Hills.'

Ishkrin threw up his hands. 'We live in a mad world,' he said. 'We have a man here who doesn't think of what is going on as an emergency.'

As Orlo walked deliberately forward, the guard officer at the entrance to the palace turned white.

'Sir,' he said, 'I have a written order here from Martin Lilgin. It came by special messenger four minutes ago. It states that, until further notice, no one is to be allowed out of, or into, Communications City.'

Orlo kept on walking. He was aware of the dozen super-scientists walking behind in the spread-out fashion they had chosen.

He said, articulating each word, 'That order is not on a legal form. And in any event, it does not apply to me, Captain. Nor does it apply to any person whom I authorize to leave here. I am the Praesidium Member by law in charge of Communications City. You understand what I am saying?'

'But –' protesting '– I have this written order in Chairman Lilgin's handwriting.'

They were now only a few feet away from each other. Orlo stopped, and showed his teeth. 'Captain, handwriting can be forged. Here, we don't operate on anything but legal procedure. So, now, I order you, you and your men will form ranks and walk ahead of us through that portion of the palace that leads to the main exit door for the employees of this section. You have thirty seconds to obey me!'

'But –'

'Move!'

There was a long pause. Then a gulp. And a salute. With that, the youth turned to the half-dozen lower ranks. 'Fall in!' he commanded, striving for sternness.

His uncertainty communicated to at least one of those lesser types. Five of the men sprang to attention. And the sixth grabbed his gun, as the others had done. However, instead of stiffening, he crouched. Up swung the rifle. It pointed at Orlo.

'No one,' he snarled, 'can order anyone to disobey The Boss. I –'

He stopped, because –

He disappeared.

Behind Orlo, the scientists broke their loose rank, and came forward into a cluster. 'Hey,' said Peter Rosten, 'which of you did that one? I always thought I had a pretty good system. But that one's better.'

There was no reply.

The dozen experts in as many sciences simply gazed at each other, and then at Orlo. But none stepped forward to take credit.

Ishkrin commented, 'Looks like whoever figured that one out doesn't want fame just yet.'

Orlo said, 'As I see it, our most important task is to make sure that we're not sniped at from a balcony or some other vantage point. So we need to divide our eyes. Two of you –' he pointed '– keep yours on our rear. Two up, two straight ahead, two left, two right.' In each case, he indicated which men for which.

The scientists merely eyed him goodhumouredly. No one moved to obey him. It was Peter Rosten who said gently, 'Orlo, don't worry about things like that. When Higenroth discovered that electricity can be made to move from one location in space to another in a simpler way than in nature, many problems in spatial relations became resolvable. I guess Lilgin was afraid to have you taught too much advanced stuff. But of course what we have goes even beyond what's out there.'

Orlo's feelings were hurt. 'Listen,' he said, 'if you characters have always been able to walk out of this prison, why didn't you leave long ago?'

'Where would we go?' asked a heavy-set man. 'In Lilginland, you have to be authorized to be wherever you are.'

It was true. And Orlo was immediately ashamed of his outburst, and of the stung feeling that had motivated it. 'There was a time in history,' he said, 'when people could seek sanctuary in church.'

'Not in Lilginland,' somebody said. 'Not in a unit of the Official Religion.'

Orlo said, 'There was a time when a man could find political sanctuary in another country.'

'Not in Lilginland earth. There are no other countries.'

'We'll probably have to do something about that,' commented Orlo, 'for the future.'

No one answered that. The men, he saw, were excited by the interior of the palace. Shocking, suddenly, to realize that these great men had never been this far out of Communications City; in fact, never been out.

They walked slowly, staring; almost as curious as children. Twice, they gathered around something as simple as an open doorway, and peered through it and beyond it. Both times, Orlo had to push at them until he got them moving again.

'Listen,' he urged, 'you're going to be entirely outside in a few minutes, if you'll just keep going.'

At the gate, he requisitioned a bus and a driver. Everybody climbed in eagerly. Yet once inside they sat timidly as the machine glided forward along a thoroughfare.

Orlo was shaken . . . Can I really believe that these people are going to take a fortress?

They walked up to the steel door of the great grey stone and steel building less than a mile from the palace. Waited while a guard phoned somebody. The youthful officer of guard presently peered at them through the steel bars. 'General Bureski will be here in a few minutes,' he said.

It was not yet quite noon. A warm wind blew along the deserted street in front of that long, high, forbidding, great grey building, which had on the wall beside the door a single, simple sign: HIGHEST POLICE.

How high could you get? . . . Orlo wondered. He deduced that the highest police did most of the political killing. Which was most of the killing.

His thought ended. Because . . . footsteps on a stone floor. A man's – and a woman's.

Orlo felt himself change colour. It couldn't be. Couldn't.

But it was.

Sheeda came out. And she stood sort of stiffly beside the grim-faced young man in uniform who had brought her.

The man said, 'The way I want this done. Tell us where she is at all times –'

'She'll be in Communications City,' said Orlo.

Bureski went on as if there had been no interruption: 'Our practical solution is that we'll decide at some later time if Lilgin is "caught". If he is, then you can keep her. If he isn't, then we'll get her back, and there will be no record of this temporary surrender.'

'Suppose,' asked Orlo, 'he speaks that word on the 'com, which you mentioned.'

'He's not in a position to observe what we do here,' said Bureski. 'We'll simply say it's done. And later on, if he wins, it will be done. And all witnesses will likewise disappear. Understand?'

'It's pragmatic,' agreed Orlo. 'Now, what about Madame Megara?'

'I've already ordered her placed in a hospital. She'll be

given protein shots, and a cosmetic job. She's been on hard labour, sir, and it'll require a month before she can even walk properly.'

'I get the picture. Which hospital?'

Bureski told him. And, with that, they separated.

In the bus back to the palace, Orlo sat beside a silent, whitefaced Sheeda. Finally, she said in a low voice, 'I was raped. I've had three men on top of me. They thought I was through; so they used me.'

'You can see,' said Orlo, 'they were not being watched on all the plastic walls on earth; so they committed what they thought would be a secret crime.'

'I thought I was through, too,' said Sheeda, 'so I enjoyed what they did. Now, I'm ashamed. There was a time when I wanted only you to have me. Do you still want that birthday present?'

'This is my birthday,' said Orlo, 'Today. And the answer is yes. We'll go to The Hills, since my secretary will probably sleep in my bed tonight. But –' he concluded '– that's hours and hours away. Before then we've got to persuade a madman that no one wants to kill him. And in fact I've got to persuade all the people who do want him dead, not to do it.'

A baffled angel face turned toward him. 'What are you talking about?' said Sheeda. 'Are you out of your mind?'

'I must be,' said Orlo frankly. 'Because at this moment I'm probably the only person in the world – except the dupes, of course – who has a compassionate feeling for Lilgin.'

He nodded, half to himself. 'It's the simplest solution, really. Keep him in power.'

TWENTY-FOUR

Eidy started to cry, as she saw Orlo walk through the door, unannounced.

'It's too much,' she wept. 'A third visit; and all three of them for nothing.'

Unheeding of her distinguished, though youthful vistor,

she ran to a connecting door; flung it open. 'Heen,' she sobbed, 'they're back again. They're back.'

It felt strangely different, hearing and seeing her in such a state, knowing this time that this pretty woman who shed such bitter tears, was his true mother.

Odd, also, to remember that the original reports had evaluated Mrs. Eidy Higenroth as a distinctly calculating young lady. (Nothing of that remained.)

Unfortunately, Orlo had no time to make an explanation. Nor, more important, dared he make one. They had come down onto the meadow near the Glucken house. As the jet landed, a scientist named Spesh, looked at his hand – at least that's what it seemed he did – and said urgently, 'Somebody's already been here. This is a trap.'

The exact analysis was that somebody's voice would trigger a device that had been planted on both Dr. and Mrs. Glucken. It was not clear what that device would do, but . . . Guess whose voice, thought Orlo – so, he merely gestured at the scientists behind him.

He stood silent, then, as the battle began . . .

The whole thing had been frantic. So many, many things to do.

Sheeda and he and his 'army' had got back to Communications City; and he had instantly had to leave her to settle down in his apartment. He, himself, hurried back into the private office.

As Orlo entered, Yuyu, whose speciality was biological aspects of electro-magnetic phenomena, jumped up and trotted forward. Whispered, 'How you feeling, kid?'

'Over-stimulated,' said Orlo truthfully.

'Still got full memory?' The big black man was intent.

'When I think about it,' said Orlo, 'I can actually hear a voice speaking faintly.'

The black looked relieved. 'Then we probably figured correct what Megara had done to you. And, of course, it makes sense.' He shrugged. 'That variant of sodium pentathol is just about all the technicians in that particular arm of the secret police would know.'

'The impression I have,' said Orlo, 'is that Higenroth connected the zygote to his equipment by way of some kind of field. As the zygote cells divided, and eventually became me, each cell retained the connection. So right now I'm connected from the top of my head to my toes.' He frowned. 'It's kind of simple. About two dozen signals – each one preceded by an emotion.'

The big Afro rubbed his hands together jubilantly. 'That's the Kirlian stuff. Hey, this I want to see in action.'

'I made the field to field test,' said Orlo. 'I looked at a man who was threatening me with a gun, did the emotion, and whispered the signal. He seemed to literally vanish.'

'Boy!' said Yuyu.

'I would guess,' said Orlo, 'since I didn't specify the connecting field, that he was moved to one or the other of two that are automatically set up. The most likely of the two is the old Higenroth workroom at the university house where he lived at that time.'

'And what's the other one?'

'At the time, I gather, the old guy –' Orlo stopped, unhappy with himself; it sounded like an unjustified colloquial way of referring to the elderly genius who had been his father; nevertheless, after a pause, he continued '– Higenroth was still toying with the idea of doing all this himself. So he had a connection with one of the Restovers of The Hills, and some idea of converting The Hills into a genuine rebel opposition to the government.' He broke off. 'That's the other place where our rifleman-guard might have ended up.'

'What's your plan?'

'Right now,' said Orlo, 'I'd better find out what's been going forward here while I was away. And then I'll outline my plan to the whole group. Okay?'

'One thousand per cent,' said Yuyu. 'The less that has to be repeated the better. But this other thing is between me and you – right?'

'Right,' said Orlo. 'Until further notice.'

He thereupon walked on into the room, and courteously greeted other men – of whom there were now eleven. Jodell said, 'We've got a bunch of women in your bedroom. And there's some other people out in the corridors, being assigned places where they can sleep on the floor.'

Orlo nodded, smiling. 'The place looked pretty packed as I came up. More coming, I presume?'

'The way we figure it,' said Jodell, 'is that all people who have any kind of access to Lilgin should be advised what's happening, and given a chance to decide where they want to be. So far they've all come here. And, of course, at our suggestion, each man has brought his wife or girlfriend. We're all waiting for that four o'clock revelation that Lilgin promised when he started to write those death sentences.'

'I have an idea,' said Orlo, 'that I should be out there doing rescue work. But, first, I'd like to tell you how, in my opinion, all this should come out.'

They couldn't seem to grasp the rationale.

'But, look,' Megura argued, 'this man has killed a billion people. Do you deny that?'

'It's probably an underestimate,' said Orlo, calmly.

'Then how can you possibly justify his remaining in power?'

'From the beginning of history,' said Orlo, 'the world seems to have been dominated by about five per cent of its males. An additional fifteen per cent could join that group, but they can't quite make it. Of the remaining 80 per cent, seven or eight are sex variants; and the remaining 70+ per cent constitute that large body of hardworking, normal people who get married and raise families and don't get divorced except for good reason. This 70 per cent, it has turned out, essentially accept a government's visible public image.

'This huge majority,' he went on, 'see all around them the good work that Lilgin has done. After all, we have to admit that the engineering approach to human nature, when viewed with the total objectivity of a cattle breeder, keeps factories and buses running, jets and rockets flying, and provides food in abundance. The population of the planet has been stabilized at slightly under three billion. People live their full lifespan free of disease, free of war, and without serious emotional problems.'

Orlo paused, shrugging. 'I'll consider that I've summarized Lilgin's good side. My point is that you and I are part of the same group of five per cent males as Lilgin. In his shoes, if you had had his power and his engineering brain, you would have done the same, or similar, depending on what your ideal is. What is the value of replacing one of that type with another of that type? That's my argument.'

He glanced at Megara. 'Sir, since you have offered

yourself as a viable substitute, what is your comment on that?'

The baby face had a look of hesitation on it. Then: 'When a man of his own free will has committed as many crimes as Lilgin, he cannot be considered for re-election.'

'This is you we're discussing. Your behaviour – if you had been in his position.'

'You're out of your mind –' roughly '– I've never harmed a living soul, except –'

'Except when?'

'Except under orders.'

'You see – you, who regard yourself as a normal person, damaged other human beings. And your excuse is you were following orders.'

'Lilgin has no excuse. He did it because he's a rat.'

Orlo shook his head. 'He did it after it finally dawned on him that he could do as he pleased because he would never be called to account, and, so long as he did most of it secretly, it would never diminish his public image.'

He saw that Megara was straining to speak; and he paused courteously. The man slashed forth this time. He said, 'Sir, you are trying to promote the biggest murderer in all history. I tell you this monster was born with rage and murder in his heart. Gentlemen, I figured it out once. Lilgin has ordered the death of 5,000 people a day *every day* of the last 190 years.'

The figure had its own impact. Orlo, who was standing, could see the effect of the total (presented in that fashion) on just about every face that he looked at. At once, there was no question. He was losing this argument.

He said hastily, 'Of that daily total, how many death orders did you, personally, transmit to the people who did the actual killing, Mr. Megara?'

The question, instead of eliciting an immediate reply, evoked an exchange of glances between Number Two and Number Three. The baby face had an appeal on it. The heavy jowls were grim.

Finally: 'Between the two of us,' said Jodell in a sardonic tone, 'I would say we transmitted about 98 per cent.'

Megara said shrilly, 'Every one of them under orders. Never by personal whim. I abhorred the whole thing. And each evening, when I sat at that table, and those images of dead women's faces, and dead men came up in my mind, I was glad Lilgin is a drunkard. Because then I could get drunk, also, and wash it all out of my mind for another night.'

'Liquor and drugs,' commented Orlo, 'were the most ancient psychotherapy. And, notice, he does it, also.'

'That bastard sat there every night, watching us, trying to loosen our tongues.'

'You said he sat there drunk.'

'Look, damn it – he didn't have to kill people to save his own rotten neck. I did – until today.'

Orlo had been flicking his gaze from face to face, as he pursued his argument. And there was no change. Megara's heated answers uttered in that deep baritone were still winning . . . Okay, okay, he thought. And changed the subject slightly.

'Mr. Megara, when you had me captured this morning, what was the procedure?'

The baby face grew calm. 'Just a form of chemical hypnosis. I wanted to make sure that Higenroth's programming was utilized properly. And so we put you under a-sodium pentathol-n. With that we brought Higenroth's signal system to the surface. And, at the key moment, when Lilgin was in that deep sleep he goes into after he has sex, I had Odette (she hates him) let us in. Whereupon, you looked at him, got the emotion, and whispered the signal – and got him on all those walls right then. So then I had the boys bring your unconscious body down here. No harm done you'll notice. Just direct action, and proper usage of the method.'

'I want to thank you for all of that,' said Orlo, 'and to tell you that your wife has been transferred to a hospital for rehabilitation, and should be in good health again in about a month.'

As he spoke those words, he saw that the blue eyes were misting again. Instead of waiting, which would have given the man time to recover, Orlo being young and still not entirely wise, plunged on. He said, 'Mr. Megara, if you replaced Lilgin, is there any basic way in which you would change the system?'

As he asked the question, it seemed as if everyone in the room except Megara stopped breathing. Megara started to answer and started to cry at the same instant. 'The details are too long to go into,' the man sobbed. 'But basically the change needed is not in the system but in administration.'

The tears were spurting wildly now. Orlo said hurriedly, 'You can prove to us that your method would not involve one man's domination?'

'Absolutely.' It was a flood of total victory.

'Thank you.' Orlo smiled a strained smile. 'You understand, gentlemen, we're just flailing at air here, so far. The most powerful dictator in the history of human existence is still sitting up there at his desk, thinking his way through all this. And I gather from those who know him that, if he comes up with a solution, it will take all factors into account, including our little conspiracy.'

His smile faded. 'So I'd better get a move on, and see if I can rescue my true mother and her husband, before one of those written death orders gets out there.'

He started for the door. 'Mr. Bylol has my jet waiting for me. I hope to be back in time to hear that four o'clock revelation . . . Yuyu, please come along this time . . .'

The battle –

The visible adversaries there in the Glucken home were a crying woman, and a tall, slender man, with Orlo slightly off to one side, and the other scientists just inside the door, waiting. There was no sign yet that Glucken was reacting to his wife's sense of doom.

The 'enemy' was a field phenomenon that had been set up to be triggered inside of the brains of two disturbed people when they heard Orlo's voice. Instantly, there would flow from them to him – something dark. (That was as much as Orlo knew.)

The super-scientist, who understood such matters, seemed to be listening, and at the same time making a tiny adjustment on a finger ring. At last, wearily – it was as if he had been working hard – the man nodded at Orlo, and said, 'When I raise my hand, then you speak – say anything. We just want your voice. There'll be a momentary shock feeling inside your brain, and then a series of thoughts and impulses. Ready?'

Orlo nodded, not exactly happy with his role. And not knowing what to expect, because . . . what kind of brain shock could they be anticipating?

The scientist, whose name was Camper, moved his hand.

Orlo said, 'Mrs. Glucken, please calm yourself, and have no fear –'

He could almost not get the final words out. His tongue started to twist in his mouth. The thought that came was like an echo of an incredibly primitive feeling: an acceptance of doom and of utter disaster. The feeling was total misery and despair. And the thought said, 'All right, I give up. Devour me!'

Almost immediately, there was a second, more distant, weaker feeling-thought (Glucken's) which said, 'To hell with all this! I don't care any more what they do. Okay, kill us!' . . . It was the same reaction, but with anger in it, not apathy.

Camper was shaking his head, wonderingly, 'I keep being amazed at these early evolutionary images. That, my friend, was the cry of an animal that has been pounced on, and is being torn to pieces; and at the ultimate moment before death is actually craving to be eaten.'

He broke off, hastily, said, 'Listen, I've had to do a reversal to save you. The cycle in a field like this has to complete. As it was set up, the power of it would have been so great it would have reached into your brain, and you would have felt the compulsion to do as their thought required: kill and eat the woman, and kill the man, violently. In order to phase out the very powerful energy flows we have here, I want you to decide in what mental state you wish to leave these two. That's the way they'll be from now on. Remember, the feelings involved in you will also be quite basic. Do the best you can for them, sir. As soon as you're ready, raise your hand; and I'll let the flow go through. But be quick, or automatic things will start to happen.'

Amazingly, a sense of personal confusion . . . The first thought: that incredible madman, Lilgin. So utterly vindictive. Twice, he's tried to get me to act against my own mother. That first day, to unknowingly place her under arrest. And now – this!

It occurred to Orlo, fleetingly, that the reaction of the two people had been singularly normal. What was happening against them had finally broken through their defences and demolished hope. And they gave up, she in her way and he in his.

Standing there, Orlo realized that his own impulses were not that normal. Worse, there was no way in these rapid moments that he could alter the intense . . . feeling . . . that was swelling up his insides. It was almost as if he felt physically bloated by it; so strong it was.

Involuntarily, he raised his hand. Instantly, he was startled by his action, and tried to lower it. And saw, shuddering, that it was too late. The deed was done.

Out of his brain had flowed a fantasy.

A child's dream.

Mother loves father, loves me. Mother will devote the rest of her life to me and to the memory of my father, Professor Higenroth.

There was an afterthought about Glucken's role: he will dedicate himself to the Higenroth ideas and theories. He will make the study that solves all this stuff in my brain about that. And will take it out of me and bring it to practical reality.

These two people, Dr. and Mrs. Glucken, she a living embodiment of a woman's timeless love for the dead genius, her first husband; he cherishing her for it, and doing everything to promote the work and genius of her murdered Higenroth . . .

TWENTY-FIVE

As the jet came down a second time, Orlo and the eleven scientists (of his original team of twelve – one man refused to fly) peered out of the small portholes – the youth had come forward to sit with the older men in the smoking compartment.

Below was another isolated house like that of the Gluckens.

Though perhaps this one was a little more sumptuous: The yard was larger. More glass glinted up at them.

'Look!' pointed one of the scientists suddenly. His speciality was a relatively obscure branch of physics having to do with an aspect of plasma relating to primitive elements – matter in an earlier form. His name was Holod.

What he pointed at alerted everybody. A long line of vehicles had emerged from a clump of trees a mile from the house. And they were now streaming along a narrow, paved road at over a mile a minute. At that speed they would arrive before anyone could get off the jet.

Orlo took one long evaluative look – and grabbed his hand mike. 'Pilot!' he yelled.

'Yes sir?' The answering voice came over the speaker system.

'Intercept those cars! Fly low! And land on the road in front of them!'

'Very well, sir.'

The jet rose, and drifted sideways. In the air its speed was unmatchable by ground machines. It spun over, and up, and around. And then floated from behind the cars, glided over them almost scraping their tops, and plunged down onto the pavement. It rolled yards only. And stopped.

Most of the cars screamed with the sounds of skidding rubber. And what happened to them in detail was never that clear to the watchers from the jet. Their attention was snatched by two automobiles that veered off the road, bounced madly, but made it around and past the great flying machine. The whole operation was so finely timed that the cars were in the yard at almost the same instant that they swerved back onto the pavement.

As they slid to a stop, doors were flung open. Several men leaped out of each vehicle, and ran toward, and into, the house.

During those moments the jet's doors were opening; and the ramps were sliding out; and there was a surge of men from many sections down each one.

But the empty feeling had come to Orlo: they were too late. Somebody had had a belated memory: what about that dumpy little grey-haired woman whom the public believes to be Lilgin's wife? . . . And so, after some talking back and forth between Megara and Jodell, waiting back in his private office, and Orlo on the jet, the great machine had changed course and flown eight hundred miles in thirty-eight minutes.

And now here it was . . . Really, he thought wearily, so little time has gone by; and so many of these orders have been transmitted by Lilgin's teenage dupes in uniform –

This might turn into a day of being one minute too late, as here, or, perhaps in other places just in time.

The sad part was that they had very little idea where most of the death orders had been sent; or why they were being sent out at all at this time.

Killing the erstwhile Mrs. Lilgin – if that's who she was – did of course have a rationale. One of the scientists had said jokingly, 'Sir –' to Orlo '– if what you say is true: that Lilgin is now going to have to settle down and behave himself. That means he's going to have to marry one of those passionate beauties and an end forever to the debauched, drunken existence that has really been his way of life.'

It had taken a moment for that to sink in; and for the memory to come: 'Hey, what about that ugly little female that –?' Long pause then: 'Listen, we'd better locate that dame. If it ever sinks in to Lilgin that he is going to have to settle down, the thought will also come that his great, duped public will expect him to settle down with her.'

Evidently, that thought had come. Whereupon, the assassins were dispatched. What was so deadly about it was that her absence would have to be explained. Therefore her murder would have to be pinned on someone. Who? And what would be the overall plot behind that?

It seemed to Orlo that he was having his first faint glimpse of the counterattack that Lilgin was mounting.

And it was already too late to stop it.

Beside Orlo, Peter Rosten said softly, 'Look at this, my friend. We've got a fix.'

He held up a shining, slightly curved metal plate about eight by ten inches. What was shining on it was a coloured picture. It was of an interior scene, very vivid and clear. In the background of a rather pretty living room stood a thickset, older woman. Facing her were seven men, all of them with drawn guns.

Orlo stared at the tableau, almost petrified. What mentally staggered him was the awful realization that the scientists had evidently tuned into the interior of that house bare moments before the kill.

He waited, holding his breath.

And then – another awareness.

The tableau was exactly that. No one in it moved. It was like a still picture, with everyone in it frozen.

A pause. And another thought. The feeling came that what he was looking at was, in its way, a parallel to a photograph that had been taken, and developed, many minutes ago. And that whatever had subsequently transpired was over and done with. He changed his question: 'What happened?' he asked.

Rosten was smiling in a pleased way. 'I have to hand it to old Doje. These Italians are sometimes hard to get along with. But he got that time stasis in there as perfect as anything I've ever seen.'

With that, he reached over. His fingers took hold of the shiny plate that Orlo held. They tugged gently. Orlo let go, silently.

'These time things can only hold so long before they get awfully sticky. We'd better get in there, and rescue, uh, she who is accepted as Mrs. Lilgin, whom that great mindless public will be expecting to see in his bedroom every night from now on.'

He finished, 'Now, is there anybody else we know about that we should rescue or let know what is happening?'

Orlo couldn't think of anyone.

But there was one individual.

TWENTY-SIX

Success raises.

Orlo glittered as he re-entered his office at exactly four minutes to four.

His question to the men waiting there produced a blank. Who else should be rescued? Obviously, everyone who had been sentenced to death. But no one knew who they were.

Jodell said, with a certain satisfaction, 'Right now, twenty-three members of the Supreme Praesidium are sitting on the floor out in the hall. The others are off on missions, and glad to be away I can tell you. Megara, any thoughts?'

The baby-faced man shook his head. He had a sour expression on that puffy face. He said unhappily, 'I have the impression, Mr. Thomas, that you're still pursuing your fantasy of maintaining Lilgin chairman.'

Orlo said breathlessly, 'It's four o'clock. I'll answer that later . . .'

Four P.M.

A smiling Lilgin looked up from his desk. If he had been shocked when his guards, a few minutes before, allowed the dumpy woman to walk in on him, it didn't show.

She was sitting, now, in a chair a few yards away. The pervasive field that had him as its centre reached out to approximately eighteen feet radius. And so, there she was, the woman who he, personally, had, long ago, after much consideration, cynically selected as the most acceptable, unenvied, middle-aged, vaguely motherly – or grandmotherly – female type. He had believed, then, that her presence would once more (as others like her had done in the past) delude all those stupes out there in the great world. Delude the men into feeling tolerantly sorry for him; and bemuse the women into something far more complex, but equally, contemptuously, tolerant.

In fact, her coming *had* changed his plan. Suddenly, he badly needed information before uttering a single word . . . What happened? How had she escaped the assassins?

But that great smile remained on the small handsome face, as Lilgin said, 'My friends, I've been getting a few reports over my ear receiver about this experiment. Despite all the assurances that were given me – that the technology had been perfected at last – it now seems that an unexpected side effect may mean that we shall have to shut off all entertainment television tomorrow, or maybe even later on this evening. Frankly, I'm not sure what's going on. If somebody comes on TV later to tell you that my statement is not so, or makes some qualifying statement, you'll have to draw your conclusions. This is what I have been told.'

The smile again. 'Maybe it will all work out. In time perhaps I will see you while you're looking at me. But I'm delaying comment until later, perhaps even until tomorrow. As you will all have observed, my wife – who has been away in her country place – is back. Right now, I want to escort her to our apartment. Naturally –' the smile widened '– you will see me do so. Such a total intimate view as you are all being allowed is a part of the experiment, which I hope you are all appreciating as much as I do . . .'

. . . Orlo said, 'So now we know. Tomorrow, he takes away their free entertainment. And he's already hinted that the technicians have mishandled this matter. Mr. Megara, do you have any analysis for us?'

'My guess is that by morning you're going to lose some of those people out there in the corridor. And by noon Jodell and I may be departing. You have the look of a sinking ship, Mr. Thomas.'

It sounded like a joke – almost. A slightly startled Orlo said, 'Before you go, would you like to hear my political theories?'

'Not really. But go ahead, if you wish.'

'We had constitutional monarchies and democracies, not because they are such great ideas, but because dictators – and dictator potentials like you and me (said Orlo Thomas, addressing Megara) – insist on it. If we trust for even one day that a "good" absolute king would just not do anything "bad," we discover that the king's cunning aide has chosen that day to exterminate everybody who might be threatening him in his control of the king's body and the king's ear. All the dictator potentials (like you and me, said Orlo to everybody) in a democracy, when they get elected are soon under pressure from their wives, their mistresses, their relatives, their friends, the business people in their constituency, and of course occasionally the people, that what they presently do is suspiciously similar to what a *de jure* dictator does. Only – in a democracy – naturally the law says they can't do it. And so the majority of them keep compromising with their natural impulse to act the role of king . . .'

Megara sneered at that point, 'One thing Lilgin and I are in total agreement on: Democracy, the most thoroughly exploded political idea that ever was. A swindle on the people from the day it was conceived. The final refuge of the Imperialist-Capitalists.'

Orlo smiled, inclined his head courteously, and went on, 'Those people who belong to the five per cent of the leader group all have an ideal. We have just heard a part of yours. Now, here's mine, which, of course, I cherish as being "the answer". When discussing an ideal, we do not ask, is it rational? We just feel it. I feel that what we need in this world are two economic systems under one government. As I would enforce this – and, being an idealist, naturally, I would enforce it – it would begin with the reinstatement of the small proprietor system.

'I visualize a government-sponsored Second Economic System – and that will be its official name. Their businesses will eventually be everywhere. They can buy land adjacent to land owned by the First Economic System. To belong to System Number Two, you must sign a release of your rights in Number One for two years at a time. Thereafter, you pay when you travel, pay for hotel and other services. We may even require that in the early stages of its development, the people in this Second System associate entirely with others like themselves by way of linked computer systems.

'Criminals in both Economic Systems will, when identified, be connected to a unitary segment of the Pervasive System, which will thereafter follow their every movement, and report to a watching computer system – which will alert the police when necessary . . . Well –' with a smile '– Mr. Megara, what do you think of my ideal?'

'I doubt if Lilgin will be interested in it.'

'So far as I can see, he's already modifying his behaviour. And so are you. Suddenly, you seem to want to be back in Lilgin's good graces. And – suddenly – you're on my side, and are willing to have him continue as leader.'

'I'm a practical man. He looks to me like he's figured out how to handle this whole situation.'

'What did he do that was so convincing to you?'

'He has different smiles. I know the winning smile; and he had it now, but not this morning.'

'In spite of our salvaging that woman whom he passes off as his wife?'

'In spite of it.'

Orlo pursed his lips. Then shook his head. 'My ideal – which, of course, I presume, derives from Professor Higenroth – says that total communication cannot be defeated.'

'Dream on, kid. He's got it figured. Right, Jodell?'

'Right.'

'That smile, right?'

'Right.' Jodell, having spoken so positively, looked over at Orlo. 'I'm sorry, Mr. Thomas, but I have to agree. We two know this man. And that smile – unmistakable.'

'What do you suggest I do?'

'I think you'd better take your scientists and make a run for it tonight.'

There was a stirring in one corner of the room, where several scientists lay on the floor. Ishkrin raised himself to a sitting position. 'We're not going. After all, here in Communications City is the only place that we're authorized to be.'

He climbed to his feet, and came over. 'Well, kid,' he said, 'it was fun while it lasted.'

'But –' Orlo protested '– everybody was so brave this morning. Now, I can only see cowardice to every horizon.'

'Orlo – that's an astoundingly bright guy up there. He's figured out an answer to total communication in about eight hours. Goodbye.'

The men began to leave, one by one. At first, Orlo was merely unbelieving. But when Yuyu came up and held out his hand, the youth said in an incredulous tone, 'How do you expect to survive, after what you and McIntosh did, except through me?'

The big black was calm. 'Take it easy, son. This is still Lilginland, but I have a feeling things will be different; and that Mac and I may not even be noticed during that transformation. So we'll just hold our breath – and hope.'

'Listen,' yelled Orlo, 'there is no answer to total communication except total perfection of character.'

The Afro kept his cool. 'Oh, he'll live with that for a while. And there may even be a few people out there who'll keep watching him every day. You heard that giveaway line, didn't you?'

'What? –' Baffled.

'About it maybe becoming a two-way look and listen?'

'That's impossible. He can't watch three billion people.'

'*We* know that, kid. But those people out there are strange. They used to believe that there was a big man up there in the sky that was keeping his eye and his ear peeled for everything they did and said. And I have a feeling that's what Lilgin has in mind for himself. The omnipotent, the omniscient. And if we here in Communications City ever break that Pervasive secret, well, my friend, I want you to visualize banks of computers doing the watching for him. And the listening.'

'I thought you scientists had decided not to work on this project for Lilgin.'

'That was yesterday. Today –' he spread his hands, expansively '– survival lies in a different direction. You keep forgetting, boy. In Lilginland you survive one day at a time.'

'I guess I had forgotten it for a minute,' said Orlo. He realized he was bracing himself in the old accepting way. He frowned. 'What about our little secret? How is that affected?'

'Today, okay. Tomorrow – who knows? Goodbye for now, or forever. I can't quite figure what's going to happen to you and that girl. But I wish you good luck.'

He started for the door.

'And I,' said Orlo, 'can't quite decide what's going to happen to you –'

He stopped. He was talking to an empty room.

After a while Sheeda came in. 'All the women,' she said anxiously, 'who were crowded into that wonderful bedroom attached to this office, suddenly got up and departed. Did I miss something?'

Orlo drew a deep breath. 'They finally agreed with me,' he said slowly, 'that Lilgin should remain as The Boss. But somehow or other the way they did it isn't the way it should have been.'

'What are we going to do?' Uneasily.

The handsome youth stared for a long time at the girl with the face of an angel, who suddenly had tears in her eyes. At last: 'We're back to living one day at a time.'

He stretched. Pounded his chest jokingly. And said with a smile, 'It doesn't really feel all that bad.'

Orlo and Sheeda spent the night at a Restover of The Hills. Their host was a chunky man in his early forties, named James Baillton. He was puzzled as to how they had suddenly gotten into his library; but then, presumably, his was a dangerous role. After they retired, he reported his suspicions to someone in the Secret Police.

The information was passed on to Bureski. 'Orlo Thomas!' said that individual. 'And did you say the girl's name is Sheeda something?'

His eyes narrowed. It wasn't too often that girls as pretty as Sheeda passed his way; not these days. So he was one of the three top men in his organization who had raped her.

He decided he was vaguely amused by what was now happening. 'Okay,' he said, 'I get the picture. Leave them alone while I think about it.'

But he was also puzzled. 'How did he get 'way out there?' Nearly eight thousand miles!

What he did, he called Lilgin. And he did all the talking, asking only for a yes or no to each question.

'. . . How *did* we get here?' asked Sheeda in the darkness, after they had made love.

'It's a field phenomenon,' Orlo explained. 'Don't worry your non-scientific little head about it.'

'But where are we?'

'We're in a Restover.'

'And what is *that*?'

Orlo explained about the phony government-controlled rebel organization called The Hills. 'You've heard of that, surely?'

'Yes, but isn't this dangerous?'

In the almost darkness, Orlo smiled. 'Well, yes. In fact, I wouldn't be too surprised if Lilgin, right now, already knows where we are. That's why I gave our real names.'

'Oh, my God!'

He turned in the bed to face her. 'Listen, my dear –' earnestly '– something is going to happen tomorrow. My own belief: Lilgin is going to get rid of most of those people. Nothing can save them. That's why I thought we'd better be out of the way.'

'B-but – if he knows where you are he'll kill you first.'

'There's a rationale about that which I'll tell you some time. Now, go to sleep!'

TWENTY-SEVEN

At 8 A.M. Lilgin stood beside one of those delicate miniature tables that made him look imposing and powerful. And he said in a grave voice:

'My friends and comrades: I have to report to you that my worst fears have been realized. I am being held a prisoner in the palace by the persons who persuaded me to launch upon this experiment in public exposure. My principal hope is that my small forces up here on the fourth floor have erected barricades. And that before those barricades are broken down, you, my good people and friends, will come in large numbers and rescue me . . .'

It was estimated afterwards that a mob of five million gathered in the streets during the course of that day. And that at least a million of them were at one time or another inside the palace itself.

Or rather, in what was left of it.

Within minutes after the speech, Orlo was doing his field to field pervasive interaction with his private office in Communications City. By that means he got Lidla, and the other girls, and even Mr. Bylol. But none of the scientists would budge.

'It goes something like this,' said Joe Ambers, lazily, as he lolled back in a chair in the library, 'this man operates on Jesuitic logic. If he thinks he needs us, he'll already have made some provision for saving us. But if he doesn't need us, then brother, there's no place on this earth that can hold us for even one day longer. Right, gentlemen?'

Several scientists who were standing by smiled their goodhumoured agreement.

'Look, you nuts!' argued Orlo, 'the character who just said that, Dr. Joe Ambers, is the person most of you believe to be a government spy. If that's even half true, then his job may be to hold you for the kill.'

No one moved. The smiles remained unchanged.

Later, when the mobs were already there, he fought his way to the library again. And through other portions of Communications City. He saw no one that he knew. Even the dead bodies that people were still stepping on had been trampled on so often that nothing recognizable remained.

Shortly after noon, an awed James Baillton came into where the refugees were gathered, and said to Orlo, 'Sir, General Bureski is on the phone.'

Bureski said, 'Listen, my friend, The Boss is going to call you in a few minutes. Here's how you talk to him . . .' It was the question, and the yes and no, technique.

'But what can he want?' whispered a white-faced Sheeda, after Bureski broke contact. 'You've done him all that damage.'

'That's the whole point,' said Orlo. 'I can't do any worse to him than I've already done. So, now he needs me.'

'He'll just torture you –' tearfully '– until you say the code word that ends the images.'

'No. That's why I brought us eight thousand miles in what appeared to be a few minutes – but was of course actually no-time. He knew last night there's a matter transmitter field situation here – and that I can escape any torture with another code word. Darling, in doing all that I lived up to my own theory of total communication. Lilgin now knows everything about me. Frankly, I think he has to keep me alive.'

During the phone call, Lilgin presently departed from the yes and no ritual and made a statement heard by all the people of earth.

He said, with his great smile, 'Orlo, these are changing times. I should tell you that I like what I have heard of your Second Economic System. I believe that it answers a need which has been becoming more apparent each passing year. I would like you to be my number one administration assistant with the task of putting such a system into effect.

'Come to see me as soon as this current turmoil subsides. You may not be aware, way up there in the mountains, that we've been having serious trouble. My two principal aides, Megara and Jodell – it turns out – have been plotting against me; for what reason I don't know. They were like brothers to me.

'Well –' smiling '– goodbye for now!'

Orlo stood up; and – he couldn't help it – he glittered.

'I'm going to act,' he said, 'as if that is the absolute truth, and –'

Orlo stopped, took a second look at something he had suddenly noticed on the wall images from the corner of his eyes. He said, abruptly, sharply, 'Who's that?'

A colourfully dressed individual had suddenly appeared in the room where the dictator was still sitting at his work desk. Several guards had followed him in. But evidently they were uncertain, and one of them said something to Lilgin.

As these matters developed, a vague memory was coming to Orlo . . . Of course, he thought, Krosco – that first night at the Praesidium dinner. The surprise arrival of such a figure had startled at the moment. And then vanished from his mind as completely as if it had never happened.

Presumably, Krosco should have been one of the people they should have thought of the day before when they were straining to recall who else should be advised of the conspiracy. He also would be worrying about *his* future.

On the wall, the dictator was waving the guards away. He seemed astonished rather than disturbed. 'Where have you been?' he asked. 'How did you get away from what happened downstairs?'

Krosco did a little dance. 'Sir,' he said, 'nobody kills a clown. They just laughed, and thought I was one of 'em, and pushed past me. But it bothered me, you not warning me!'

Lilgin leaned back in his chair. He seemed undecided for a moment. But it was clear from his next words that he was remembering that, historically, the Court Fool had occasionally been used to transmit messages. 'Did anybody send you?' he asked. 'And, if so, what do they want?'

Krosco who had brought a cap gun and a papiermâché sabre, pointed the gun and fired it directly at the dictator's face. Since it was the kind of madly sensible thing that a Fool does – matching the exact fear in the victim – the Great Man jumped. And then as he realized it really was a cap pistol, he started to laugh hysterically. He was still laughing when the papiermâché sabre – which turned out to be razor-sharp metal alloy – swung through the air and sliced off his head.

Also by A. E. Van Vogt in Sphere Science Fiction

THE SECRET GALACTICS

Reality twisted . . . slightly. Earth shivered. For a split second the Solar System wasn't. And then was again. Less than a billionth of a second – but a time shift had nonetheless happened.

As the shadow ship started to emerge from the time jump, men and aliens were locked in a secret, undeclared war for control of the Earth. Genetically altered, the aliens looked exactly like humans. And they were in positions of power everywhere. Opposing them were two humans and one isolated brain in a mechanical body. But between them they held the one secret that the aliens had never learned about the people of Earth. . . .

THE UNIVERSE MAKER

Morton Cargill was very drunk when he crashed the Chevrolet into a tree, killing his girl passenger. But he was stone-cold sober when, a year later, that same girl turned up, as real as he was, and calmly informed him that the Inter-Time Society for Psychological Adjustments had arranged for him to be murdered, to atone for her own death. As if that wasn't bizarre enough, Cargill escaped from the Society's clutches only to find himself in a far future where three conflicting societies struggled for dominance. There were the Floaters, a race of aerial vagabonds; the Tweeners, who plotted world conquest; and the insubstantial Shadows, who were as secretive and sinister as their name suggested. Each faction had a purpose – and, whether he liked it or not, each purpose involved Morton Cargill. . . .

As well as THE UNIVERSE MAKER, this volume also contains A. E. Van Vogt's novella THE PROXY INTELLIGENCE.

0 7221 8733 5 75p

MISSION TO THE STARS

In the far distant future, the spaceship *Star Cluster* is searching for certain inhabited planets lost somewhere in the teeming wilderness of outer space. The inhabitants of these planets know the ship is searching for them, but they refuse to reveal their location. Why don't these people want to be found? What is their secret? Discover the astounding answers as you read this gripping, classic tale of interstellar adventure by A. E. Van Vogt, one of the all-time great names in adventurous science fiction.

0 7221 8775 0 60p

THE WORLD OF NULL-A

Gosseyn himself didn't know his own identity – only that he could be killed, yet live again. But someone knew who Gosseyn was, and was using him as a pawn in a deadly game that spanned the galaxy!

0 7221 8746 7 65p

THE PAWNS OF NULL-A

Gosseyn knew the creature threatened to destroy the whole solar system, but not even his Null-A-trained double brain could thwart the Follower's plans. Then he found himself face-to-face with a force that lay at the very roots of human intelligence . . . all the while fighting his own insane mind.

0 7221 8747 5 65p

Also available from Sphere Books

SCIENCE FICTION: THE GREAT YEARS
Carol and Frederick Pohl (Eds.)

In this superb anthology, Carol and Frederick Pohl present some of the most outstanding stories from the 30's, 40's and 50's – the 'Golden Years' of science fiction. This collection of trailblazers takes off in style with Eric Frank Russell's "And Then There Were None" and goes by way of such all-time greats as William Tenn's "The Liberation of Earth" and Frederic Brown's "Placet is a Crazy Place" to C. M. Kornbluth's classic "The Little Black Bag". Other past favourites included are "Old Faithful" by Raymond Z. Gallun, James MacCreigh's "Wings of the Lightening Land" and H. L. Gold's "A Mother of Form".

0 7221 6294 8 75p